THIR

THR(

ADITYA NARAYAN Dhₒ....   ' and
educated at the Doon School and the universities of .... and
Oxford. He spent many years as a career diplomat, and went on to
become India's High Commissioner to Kenya and the Seychelles, and
later the Ambassador to Portugal and Yugoslavia. He has translated
various classics from the Sanskrit, including the plays of Bhasa (*The
Shattered Thigh and Other Plays*), Dandin's *Daśa Kumāra Charitam* (*Tales of
the Ten Princes*) and Nārāyana's *Hitopadeśa*, all published by Penguin.

SIMHĀSANA DVĀTRIMŚIKĀ

Thirty-two Tales of
The Throne of Vikramaditya

Translated from the Sanskrit with an introduction by
A. N. D. HAKSAR

PENGUIN BOOKS

PENGUIN BOOKS

Published by the Penguin Group
Penguin Books Ltd, 80 Strand, London WC2R 0RL, England
Penguin Group (USA) Inc., 375 Hudson Street, New York, New York 10014, USA
Penguin Group (Canada), 90 Eglinton Avenue East, Suite 700, Toronto, Ontario, Canada M4P 2Y3
(a division of Pearson Penguin Canada Inc.)
Penguin Ireland, 25 St Stephen's Green, Dublin 2, Ireland (a division of Penguin Books Ltd)
Penguin Group (Australia), 250 Camberwell Road, Camberwell,
Victoria 3124, Australia (a division of Pearson Australia Group Pty Ltd)
Penguin Books India Pvt Ltd, 11 Community Centre,
Panchsheel Park, New Delhi – 110 017, India
Penguin Group (NZ), cnr Airborne and Rosedale Roads, Albany,
Auckland 1310, New Zealand (a division of Pearson New Zealand Ltd)
Penguin Books (South Africa) (Pty) Ltd, 24 Sturdee Avenue,
Rosebank, Johannesburg 2196, South Africa

Penguin Books Ltd, Registered Offices: 80 Strand, London WC2R 0RL, England

www.penguin.com

First published by Penguin Books India 1998
Published in Penguin Classics 2006
1

Printed in England by Clays Ltd, St Ives plc

ISBN-13: 978-0-140-45517-5
ISBN-10: 0-140-45517-5

P.M.S.

For
Vikram and Annika
with love

Key to the Pronunciation of Sanskrit Words

Vowels:

The line on top of a vowel indicates that it is long.

a	(short)	as the u in but
ā	(long)	as the a in far
i	(short)	as the i in sit
ī	(long)	as the ee in sweet
u	(short)	as the u in put
ū		as the oo in cool
e		is always a long vowel like the a in mate
ai		as the i in pile
o		as the ow in owl

Consonants:

k, b ans p are the same as in English
kh is aspirated

g	as in goat
gh	is aspirated
j	as in jewel
jh	is aspirated
ṭ	and ḍ are hard when dotted below as in talk and dot
ṭṭ	is the aspirated sound
ḍḍ	is aspirated
ṇ	when dotted is a dental; the tongue has to curl back to touch the palate
n	as in king
t	undotted is a soft sound in thermal
th	is aspirated
d	undotted is a soft sound—there is no corresponding English sound, the Russian 'da' is the closest.
dh	is aspirated

ph and bh are aspirated

Apart from s as in song, and sh as in shore, Sanskrit has a third sibilant, ś which is similar to the second, e.g. Śiva. Ch is pronounced as in cello and chh as in chhota. Words and names in common usage have been spelt without diacriticals.

Contents

Introduction

*V*ikramaditya is a famous figure in Indian folklore. He is represented as a great and good king whose reign was a golden age of righteousness, peace and prosperity. This image has persisted in popular memory for at least a thousand years.

The aura of virtue, might and splendour surrounding the persona of Vikramaditya was such that many Indian rulers assumed this name as a title. Boys today continue to be named Vikram, Vikrama, or Bikramjit, if not given the full appellation which means, literally, 'the sun of valour'. An era bearing the king's name, which was already current in India when the Central Asian scholar Alberuni visited the country[1] at the turn of the millennium, remains in use to this day. And Ujjain, a town in the state of Madhya Pradesh identified with Vikramaditya's fabled capital Ujjayini, still has several sites associated with him, apart from being the seat of a new Vikram University.

Myths and traditions often contain kernels of actual history, and many scholars consider that behind the legends of Vikramaditya there must be a historical figure who ruled at Ujjayini and founded an era. Some historians tried to identify him with the Gupta emperor Chandragupta II, who had the title Vikramaditya, and whose reign was one of the high watermarks of ancient Indian culture; but this monarch lived some four hundred years after the commencement of the Vikrama Era in 58-57 BC. Another academic opinion holds it possible that later rulers who assumed the same name, such as Chandragupta II, may have been confused with the original Vikramaditya in the popular legends that have grown around this figure.[2] In any event, the force of these perennial stories is such that the ancient king appears, along with great historical rulers such as Aśoka and Akbar, in the illuminated panels prepared[3] for the original calligraphed document of the Constitution of modern India. His depiction there has been reproduced on the cover of the present volume.

✤

The numerous stories about Vikramaditya form a considerable literature in Sanskrit, from which some of them passed into other Indian languages. In turn at least one was rendered into Sanskrit from Maharashtri Prākrit. The Sanskrit works still extant date mostly from the medieval period. They include: the *Mādhavānala Kathā* of Ānanda, about the adventures of two lovers eventually united with each other through the king's chivalrous efforts; the *Vikramodaya*, in which he appears in the guise of a wise parrot; the *Panchadaṇḍa Chhatra Prabandha*, containing tales of magic and witchcraft; and the *Vīra Charitra* of Ananta, which begins with Vikramaditya's final war, and continues with his successors.[4] An interesting work is the Jaina story *Kālakāchārya Kathānaka*,[5] which tells incidentally of the king's conquest of Ujjayini and founding of a new era. But the two most popular works are the *Vetāla Panchaviṃśatikā* or the Twenty-five Tales of the Vampire, and the *Simhāsana Dvātriṃśikā* or the Thirty-two Tales of the Throne. The former has been translated into English many times, beginning with the rendition by Sir Richard Burton of Arabian Nights fame in the nineteenth century.[6] The latter, presented here, has received comparatively less attention.

The Vetāla tales are essentially stories ending in

riddles, told to King Vikramaditya to test his wisdom. The Simhāsana tales, on the other hand, are stories about the king himself. They describe his merits and exploits, his birth, accession, rule and death. They are, moreover, intended to edify as well as to entertain. The king is depicted as a paragon of virtue, and his deeds as models of noble and heroic, magnanimous and courageous conduct.

The *Simhāsana Dvātrimśikā* has a colourful setting of adventures and miracles. At its centre is the royal throne or *simhāsana* of Vikramaditya, supported by *dvātrimśat* or thirty-two statues of celestial nymphs. The first six frame stories narrate the circumstances of Vikramaditya's accession after the abdication of his half-brother; his receiving the magic throne from the king of the gods; and his last battle and death, after which the throne was hidden as there was no one worthy of occupying it. The later frame stories describe the subsequent discovery of the throne by King Bhoja of Dhārā and his attempts to ascend it, which occasion the thirty-two tales of the throne.

Each time Bhoja starts to mount the throne, one of the thirty-two statuettes comes to life and interrupts him with a tale of the deeds of Vikramaditya, illustrative of the latter's virtues, especially his heroism and generosity. Each tale ends with the admonition that Bhoja may sit on the throne if he can match the merits of the earlier king. After thus restraining him thirty-two times, the nymphs explain in the epilogue how they came to be transfixed to the throne as the result of a curse from which they are now released. Bhoja then installs the throne in a shrine as an object of reverence.

Though full of miraculous happenings, the stories also describe various human predicaments. A king is cuckolded (II)[7]; another must punish his own son (tale 31); a young man loses his friends along with his wealth (tale 12); the hero must choose between protecting his reputation and helping his rival (tale 24). There is a recurring pattern of Vikramaditya obtaining some priceless gift as a result of his extraordinary heroism, and then giving it away in a supreme gesture of generosity or compassion. A sequence of changing backgrounds provides rich variety to this constant theme. The scenes of individual stories shift from a coronation ceremony (tale 1) to a pleasure park in spring time (tale 6); from a great temple (tale 8) to a courtesan's house (tale 9); and from occult rituals (tale 17) to the royal routine (tale 23). For additional colour there are battles with ogres (tale 12), human sacrifices (tale 28), divine dancers (V., tale 19), a magic show (tale 30), and the hero's visits to other worlds (tale 18, 19). Two stories (IV, tale 31) interestingly recapitulate the plot of the *Vetāla Panchaviṃśatikā*. One story (Appendix) appended to a few manuscripts of the text describes Vikramaditya's supernatural birth.

Narrative energy and diversity is heightened by the geographical sweep of the stories. Action normally begins and ends in the royal capital Ujjayini, also called Avanti. But it ranges from Kanchi (tale 9) in the south to Kashmir (tale 8) in the north, and from Gujarat (Appendix) in the west to Assam (tale 22) in the east. In between there is mention of the regions of Andhra, Karnataka and Mālava; cities like Dhārā and Pratishṭhāna; and centres of pilgrimage like Kedāra and Vārāṇasī, Prayāga and Gayā. These references also provide a dual framework of geographical awareness and of cultural identity at the time when the stories were composed.

❖

The credit for preparing the presently definitive critical edition of the *Simhāsanā Dvātriṃśikā* in its different recensions goes to the American Sanskritist Franklin Edgerton, whose labours also included literal translations of these recensions, their comparative analysis, and the compilation of a critical apparatus. This pioneering work[8], completed in 1917 and published nine years later by Harvard University, has remained the standard reference point for any further study of the subject, including that presented here.

In the course of his investigations Edgerton found the work titled variously in different manuscripts. The titles referred to the king, the throne, the divine statues, the number thirty-two, or a combination of these features. Some of the titles were: *Simhāsana Dvātriṃśikā* or *Dvātriṃśatikā; Dvātriṃśat Puttalikā Ākhyāna* (Thirty-two Statue Stories); *Vikrāmaditya Simhāsana Dvātriṃśikā* (Thirty-two Tales of the Throne of Vikramaditya); and *Vikramaditya* or *Vikrama Charita* (Deeds or Adventures of Vikrama). Edgerton chose the last of these arbitrarily as the title of his own work, as it was the shortest and the simplest. Later scholars[9] have considered the first-mentioned title as more appropriate. It also reflects the folk roots of the stories, whose Hindi and Newari versions from north India and Nepal are known respectively as the *Singhasan Bateesi* and the *Batisa Putrika Katha.* This title has as such been used here also.

Edgerton dubbed his editions of the four major recensions of the *Simhāsana Dvātrṃśika* the Southern (SR), the Metrical (MR), the Brief (BR), and the Jainistic (JR) recensions. He also examined another recension from Bengal, but considered it an adaptation of JR, to which it was very similar. The texts of SR and MR have been found almost entirely in southern India, while those of BR and the more common JR originate in the north. None of them is held in some scholarly opinion to be the ur-text of the work,[10] though SR is thought to come closest to it.[11]

The main thread of the narrative is the same in all the recensions, though verbally they are distinct. As compared to SR, the order of the stories is often changed in JR, and occasionally in MR and BR. Some of the incidental stories are omitted in BR, and some different stories appear only in JR. While MR is composed entirely in verse, the other three are in prose interspersed with gnomic and descriptive stanzas. BR, as the name implies, is a somewhat summarized and abbreviated version; JR contains recapitulatory stanzas at the beginning or end of each story; and SR is the lengthiest of all recensions. An important distinction is that JR projects Jaina religious and ethical beliefs, while the other three recensions manifest orthodox Hindu perspectives in their references to deities and religious observances. Edgerton's analysis of the texts claimed that 'JR too was derived from the orthodox archetype of SR, MR and BR',[12] and its didactic and sententious emphasis in particular was enhanced under the growing socio-cultural influence of Jainism.[13]

Nothing is known about the author of the original *Simhāsana Dvātrimśikā*, and very little about the compilers or redactors of individual recensions. Some manuscripts of JR indicate in identical stanzas that it was rendered from an earlier Mahārāshtri Prākrit version into Sanskrit by Kshemānkara Muni, seperately identified as a Śvetāmbara Jaina teacher who also authored another work called *Shatpurusha Charita*. Some other JR manuscripts attribute authorship to Siddhasena Divākara or Ramachandra Suri. No other recension contains any of these names. One manuscript of SR names the author as Kālidāsa, one of the MR mentions Nandiśvara, and the name Vararuci is found in some Bengal recensions. It is evident that none of these names can by themselves solve the question of original authorship; most probably they refer only to the scribes or the redactors of the manuscripts concerned.[14]

The evidence is better for dating the work. All the stories are narrated to King Bhoja of Dhārā who is a historical figure. Also known from other sources as a scholar and a patron of learning, he reigned from about

1018 to 1055 AD. It was earlier thought[15] that the *Simhāsana Dvātrimśikā* was perhaps composed in Bhoja's honour during his rule. However the various recensions were found to contain references to or quotations from later Sanskrit works such as the *Chaturvarga Chintāmaṇi* of Hemādri, the *Rati Rahasya* of Kokkoka, the *Sarva Darsana Samgraha* of Madhava, and the *Prabandha Chintāmaṇi* of Merutunga. These date the *Simhāsanā Dvātrimśikā's* composition to the end of the thirteenth or the beginning of the fourteenth century AD.[16] The legend of Vikramaditya is of course a thousand years older, the title having been used as early as the fourth century. It is also possible that the throne stories had been current well before they were first textually compiled.

As with many other works of *Kathā* or story literature, the *Simhāsana Dvātrimśikā* also incorporates didactic and descriptive verses from various sources. Apart from those mentioned in the preceding paragraph, these sources include the two great epics; various purāṇas like the Garuḍa and the Skanda; famous *Kāvya* works like Kālidāsa's *Śakuntalā, Kumāra Sambhava* and *Mālavikāgnimitra*, and Māgha's *Śiśupālavadha*; and verse anthologies like those of Amaru and Bhartrihari. The commonest sources for its quotations, specially in SR, are the verse collections on policy and conduct named after Chāṇakya and, to a lesser extent, verses from the *Panchatantra* and the *Hitopadeśa*. Its own contents, in turn, have provided quotations in later works like the *Mādhavānala Kathā* and the *Kathā Ratnākara*.[17]

Such literary activity sheds an interesting light on the use and status of Sanskrit at the time. By the thirteenth century Sanskrit had already been supplanted by Persian as the official language in many north Indian kingdoms, and the use of regional languages was also on the increase with the spread of the *bhakti* movement. Recent histories of the period note that this did not result in the discontinuance of writing in Sanskrit;[18] but its usage was confined to court and priestly circles in kingdoms still outside Turkish and Afghan rule. However, works like the *Simhāsana Dvātriṃśikā* indicate not only the persistent impact of earlier literature, but also the existence of a wider audience for this type of Sanskrit composition which, with its tales of magic and fantasy in simple language, presupposes a more popular appeal. Another reason for this particular work's popularity was doubtless its evocation of an earlier golden age at a time of turmoil and foreign invasions which had penetrated as far as southern India by the beginning of the fourteenth century. Tale 25 is a good example.

The didactic emphasis in the *Simhāsana* stories, and their repeated and sometimes exaggerated depictions of moral behaviour, has led to some modern criticism that they are tedious and unattractive. Edgerton complained of 'a certain monotony and flatness' in some of them, and the European Indologist Ludwik Sternbach expressed the view that the collection 'unjustly enjoys a good reputation, a reputation greater than its literary worth justifies'.[19]

There may be differing opinions on the literary merit of the *Simhāsana Dvātriṃśikā*, but its popularity over the centuries is demonstrated by the large number of old manuscripts of various recensions in which it exists. Edgerton's own work utilized thirty-three manuscripts originating in different parts of India over a period of nearly four hundred years, if not longer. Another fourteen manuscripts sent from Bombay were lost in the shipwreck of the *Titanic*. That Indians valued ethical exhortation in their literature is evident from the regard in which the great epics, the *jātaka* tales and the *subhāshita* verses have been held over the ages. One function of good literature was to provide knowledge of right conduct, as expressed in the dictum *vyavahāra vide* of the celebrated eleventh-century Kashmiri critic Mammata. The Simhāsana tales too, in the words of the modern scholar Saroja Bhate,[20] are 'a good illustration of the use of the story for moral instruction'. Narrative didacticism is however balanced by stylistic lucidity and arresting backgrounds.

The *Simhāsana Dvātriṃśikā* is known to have been translated into Persian by order of the emperor Akbar in about 1574 AD. The Persian version was rendered into French in 1817, bringing the work to the West for the first time. It also exists in Siamese, Newari and Tibetan or Mongolian versions, as well as in adaptations in various Indian languages such as Bengali, Gujarati, Hindi, Tamil and Telugu.[21] The only translation so far from the original Sanskrit into English has been Edgerton's literal rendering over eighty years ago, to which reference has already been made.[22]

The present translation is intended to bring this venerable classic before today's general readership in modern English. I have prepared it from the Sanskrit texts edited by Edgerton, and also profited from his critical apparatus and explanations of obscure terms. His layout of the four recensions in horizontally parallel sections, which facilitated the selection and arrangement of the text for this translation, has been of particular utility.

Edgerton had also attempted a reconstruction of the original form of the *Simhāsana Dvātriṃśikā* from its various recensions. Later scholarship considered[23] that attempt unconvincing, and suggested that the archetype of the existing recensions can be established only on the basis of an ur-text which is yet to be discovered. In assembling material for the present translation, I have made no effort to repeat the earlier exercise. I have also refrained from presenting separate translations of the four recensions, as these already exist and the exercise would involve considerable narrative repetition, which may be tedious for the general reader. Instead, I have endeavoured to bring within a single framework a combination of the different recensions, which would together present the story of Vikramaditya and his throne in its fullest colour and detail.

The present translation draws mainly from the texts of SR, MR and JR, apart from some details taken from BR. Some stories are taken entirely from single recensions. For example, tales III and 29 occur only in JR from where they are taken; the first provides an account of the king's accession not given elsewhere, and the second gives a complete story unlike its counterparts in other recensions, which contain mainly panegyrics. Tale 2 and the emboxed story in tale 3 are taken from MR, where they occur in greater detail. Tale 28 about the human sacrifice is drawn from SR for the same reason. The famous tale about the fruit of immortality in II is also from SR, except for one line from JR which provides the interesting information that Vikramaditya had been exiled during the reign of his predecessor Bhartrihari—some later works say at the instigation of the latter's lustful wife.

Some other portions are drawn largely from one recension. Two-thirds of the Prologue is from SR, while its last paragraph is taken from JR. The tale of the Image of Poverty in tale 32, which Winternitz[24] considered the wittiest of all, only occurs in JR, but its first two introductory paragraphs are from MR. The introductory portions of all but six[25] of the thirty-two tales of the throne are taken from MR where their language is more diverse as compared to the other recensions. In the remaining sections of the present translation, the Sanskrit text has been drawn from different recensions and combined to produce a cohesive whole. The Appendix contains the story of the birth of

Vikramaditya. This is found in some manuscripts of JR, but is generally considered a later addition in less refined language.

The four recensions vary in their linguistic style. SR is the simplest, but expansive and sometimes prolix. It also has the largest number of interspersed hymnal, gnomic and descriptive stanzas. The language of JR is more crisp and embellished, while BR is a summary which nevertheless gives some interesting details, like the king staying naked to protect the cow with his own clothes (tale 26). MR is composed mainly in the *śloka* metre, and contains some elaborate descriptions in the *kāvya* manner. No attempt has been made in the present work to replicate these stylistic variations, or to reflect the double meanings and other figures of speech popular in literary Sanskrit, which occur chiefly in MR and JR. Nor have the interspersed stanzas been treated differently apart from presenting them in a distinctive form for separate identification; some have been excluded to avoid repetition. My endeavour has been to produce a prose translation of the whole in contemporary language which may convey some of the colour and the flavour of the original, as well as its smooth flow, while maintaining fidelity to its text.

The king has the names Vikramaditya, Vikramārka or Vikrama in the original. The first two are synonyms, and the second name has therefore been excluded from this translation. The other two have been used as they occur in the original. Another epithet for the king excluded here is Sāhasānka, which means 'marked by courage'. Intrepidity is perhaps the basic feature of Vikramaditya's personality projected in these stories, underlying his innate dignity and magnanimity. It is summed up best in tale 32, the final tale of the throne.

❖

I first encountered the Vikramaditya stories in Hindi as a boy, and retain from that time an impression of the king's wonderful nonchalance, which never seemed to be affected by others repeatedly taking advantage of it. The Sanskrit original now translated came to my notice much later through Parsa Venkateshwar Rao Jr. of *Indian Express*, whom I would like to thank here for the introduction. I read it with much pleasure at the simple but vivid language and portrayals of the stories and admiration for Edgerton's scholarly editing. There was also, I must add, a further element of personal interest: my wife and I had meanwhile become parents of a son we named Vikram. Though the name had been selected more for reasons of euphony and meaning than of history, it was still a satisfying experience to learn about the merits of its original bearer through the *Simhāsana Dvātriṃśikā*. This book is now dedicated to Vikram and his wife Annika with the hope that it will remind them and their progeny of the good deeds it describes.

I would like to thank David Davidar, Editor and Chief Executive Officer of Penguin Books India for giving me extended time to complete this translation; Udayan Mitra for his overall cooperation; Smriti Vohra and Anjana Ramakrishnan for editing the typescript. I am grateful to H.K. Kaul, Librarian of New Delhi's India International Centre, for showing me the Vikramaditya panel in the Constitution of India, and to his colleagues, Sushma Zutshi and Vijaya Murthy, for assistance in locating reference material. The one person who has helped me more than anyone else in the preparation of this book is my wife Priti, for whom no words can ever be adequate.

Vikrama Samvat 2055   A.N.D.H.
November 1998
New Delhi

PART I

1. Prologue

 $\mathcal{S}$ alutation to the great Ganeśa[1],
remover of dark obstacles,
whose gaze is tender
with limitless compassion.

Having done reverence
to Vishnu the Primal Being,
Brahmā the Lotus-Born,
Śiva the Lord of Umā,
and the blessed Sarasvati,[2]
I write of the deeds of Vikramaditya.

Once Parameśvara, the Supreme Lord, was seated on the peak of Mount Kailāsa. Jagadambikā, the Mother of the World, bowed to him and said: 'Behold,

The wise pass their time in the pleasures
of literature and the sciences.
Others, who are fools, spend it
in sleeping or quarrelling.[3]

To pass the time in keeping with this maxim, tell a tale which will fill every mind with wonder.'

'Listen, my beloved,' Parameśvara replied, 'I will tell a tale which will entrance every heart.

'Once upon a time thirty-two most marvellous tales were recounted before the estimable King Bhoja, a repository of the most excellent royal glory. Related by the thirty-two statuettes supporting a throne of moonstone gems built by some god, these tales extolled the virtues of the noble Vikramaditya. Now, those who wish to know may ask: "Whose throne was it? By whom and to whom was it given? How did Bhoja obtain it? What are these stories?" So, listen to one who will explain all this.'

※

II. King Bhartrihari and the Fruit of Immortality

*T*here is a city called Ujjayini. It lacked nothing: it was better even than Indra's heaven. In it there reigned a king called Bhartrihari, who was versed in all the arts and skilled in every science. All the nobles and the lords paid him homage: the vermilion from the hair-partings of their wives reddened his feet. His own wife, Anangasenā, was more beautiful and charming than the nymphs of heaven. He also had a younger brother named Vikramaditya whose valour was greater than that of all his enemies. But he had been exiled in disgrace for some reason since the time of the king's coronation.

In this city there was a brahmin who was an adept in all the sciences, specially that of incantations. But he was exceedingly poor. He propitiated the goddess Bhuvaneśvari with a ritual of spells and charms, and she asked him to make a wish.

'Goddess,' the brahmin cried, 'if you are pleased with me, grant me freedom from old age and death'. The goddess gave him a divine fruit, saying, 'My son, you will never grow old or die after you eat this fruit.'

The brahmin took the gift and went home. He bathed and did his devotions. Then, as he sat down to eat the celestial fruit, a thought crossed his mind. 'What am I doing?' he asked himself. 'I am so poor. Whom will I benefit by becoming immortal? Though I live for ever, I

will still be a beggar. Even a short life is preferable if one
can do some good to others. It is worthwhile only if one
acquires learning, wealth and other merits, even though
one lives for no more than a moment. As it is said:

His life is fruitful, say the sages,
who lives acclaimed for learning,
valour, wealth and other merits.
For even a crow can live long,
eating leftovers.

The crow lives long, gobbling putrid leftovers.
One truly lives, who does so
with righteousness and renown.

He really lives, by whose living
many others live too.
For, does not even a stork
fill its own belly with its beak?

There are thousands of petty people,
engaged in filling their own bellies.
That person alone stands out in virtue,
who regards his own interest
as serving that of others.
The submarine fire
consumes the ocean
only to satisfy itself;
the cloud does it in order
to rain upon a world
oppressed by summer's heat.

A man whose life, actions and qualities
have no worthwhile meaning
is like a word formed at random,
no more than a name.[1]

'Therefore this fruit should be given to the king. He will then be freed from death and ageing, and be able to protect and nurture all the four castes as it should be rightly done.'

Taking the fruit, the brahmin then went to Bhartrihari.

'O King, may the gods Hara,
who sports the serpent garland,
and Hari, who wears
the yellow garment, bless you.'

With this benediction he placed the fruit in the king's hands and said: 'Majesty, I obtained this incomparable fruit as a mark of divine grace. Eat it, and you will become immune to old age and death.'

The king took the fruit, and dismissed the brahmin with many gifts. 'I will become immortal by eating this fruit,' he pondered, 'but I love Anangasenā deeply. She will die while I still live, and I will not be able to bear the pain of that separation. So, I will give this fruit to her instead, for she is dearer to me than life.'

He then called the queen and gave her the fruit. Now she had taken a stablehand as her lover and, after some thought, she gave the fruit to him. He passed it on to a servant maid who was his sweetheart. She in turn gave it to a cowherd with whom she was in love. The cowherd was deeply in love with a girl who carried the cowdung, and he presented the fruit to her.

The dung carrier would collect the cattle droppings and take them out of the village. She put the basket of dung on her head, flung the fruit on top of it, and came out thus on the highway. At that time King Bhartrihari was going on a hunt with the princes. He noticed the fruit lying on top of the excrement on the girl's head. Taking it, he turned back and went home. Then he summoned the brahmin.

'O brahmin,' he asked, 'is there another fruit of the kind you presented to me?' The brahmin replied: 'My lord, that was a celestial fruit obtained as a gift from a god. There is no other fruit like it on earth. One may not lie to the king who too is a god personified and must be regarded as such.

The sages declare that the king
is an embodiment of all the gods.
A wise man should look upon him
as such, and speak no lies before him.'

'Well,' said the king, 'what if another fruit like that one were to be here?'

'Didn't you eat it?' the brahmin asked.

'I did not eat it,' the king admitted, 'I gave it to my beloved Anangasenā.'

'Then ask her if she ate it.'

The king called Anangasenā, put her under oath, and questioned her. She acknowledged that she had given the fruit to the stablehand. The latter was summoned and asked, and he said that he had given it to the servant maid. She said that she gave it to the cowherd, and he that he had presented it to the cowdung carrier.

When the truth dawned upon him, the king was overcome by a deep depression. He recited a stanza:

'In vain do men delude themselves
with the youth and beauty of lovely women.
Kāma[2] is king in their hearts,
and does exactly what he pleases.

'No one, alas, can understand what women think and do. It is said,

Even the gods cannot anticipate
the bucking of a horse

and the thundering of a cloud;
the hearts of women
and the fate of man;
and if it will rain excessively
or not at all. How then can man?

Further,

Men may catch a tiger in the forest,
a bird in the air, or a fish
in the middle of the river.
But they can never gauge
the fickle minds of women.

What is more,

Flowers may rain from the sky,
and a barren woman's son
may reign as king.
·Such things can come to pass,
but women's hearts can never
be straightforward.

And,

The wiles of women delude
even those savants who understand
joy and sorrow, victory and defeat,
life and death.

What is more,

Even those with no ulterior motive
say that it is in the nature
of all women to want another man
even though they already have one
just like Kāma, the god of love.

Women can hoodwink a man
in a moment, even one
with a wealth of wisdom.
And they do it without spells
or incantations, religious rites
or modest manners.

I believe that the lover
preferred by women is generally
one who has been thrown out
of his family and clan,
a vile, wicked and base person,
who should be shunned.

They may have dignity, and prestige
and many laudable merits;
but women fall into wicked ways
on their own, for no reason at all.

They laugh and weep
for the sake of lucre;
they make men trust them,
and themselves trust no one.
Such women should always be avoided
by men of good family and character,
just like the rice cakes
which are left in cemeteries.

No fortune is greater than renunciation,
no happiness more than enlightenment,
no saviour other than Hari, and
no enemy worse than this worldly round.'

Reciting this last stanza, Bhartrihari renounced the world
and himself retired to a forest.

*

III. Vikrama wins the Kingdom

*L*eft without a ruler, the kingdom of Avanti, of which Ujjayini was the capital, came to be dominated by a genie named Agnivetāla. Each time the ministers installed a new king, the genie would kill him the same night. There seemed no way to stop him, and the courtiers were at a loss as to what could be done.

At this time Vikramaditya returned from abroad. No one could recognize him as he came in the guise of a common man. He enquired from the ministers why the kingdom was rulerless. They told him about the problem caused by the genie.

'Then, make *me* the king today,' Vikrama said to the ministers. And, thinking that here was someone with heroic qualities who might be able to save the situation, they installed him as king straightaway.

Vikrama carried out the role of king all day. In the evening he had a sacrificial offering with many gifts placed. beside his bed, and himself sat up keeping vigil. In due course the genie came. He was deadly and terrifying to look at as he towered above, staring at all the gifts and offerings. Then, as he drew his scimitar and advanced for the kill, Vikrama spoke up: 'Wait!' he cried, 'take the offering first. Then I too will be at your disposal.'

The genie took the offering and was content. 'O hero,' he said to Vikrama, 'I give this kingdom to you. But you must provide me a sacrificial offering every day.' With

these words he departed. In the morning, when the
ministers saw that the king was still alive and well, they
were delighted and said: 'He is truly a prince among
heroes.'

The genie would now come daily and take the offered
gifts. One day the king asked him: 'How great is your
power, genie, and how much do you know?'

'I can do whatever I please,' the genie replied, 'and I
know everything.' The king then asked: 'How long will I
live?' 'A hundred years,' said the genie. 'But there is a gap
in my life,' the king said, 'so, can you increase or reduce
it by one year?' To this the genie responded: 'No one at
all can make your life longer or shorter than what is
ordained,' and he took the gifts and went away.

When the genie returned on the following day, he
noticed that the king had not put out any gifts whatsoever
for him. 'Why have you not prepared the gifts today?' he
asked angrily. Vikrama said: 'If no one at all can increase
or reduce my life, then why should I carry out a sacrifice
for you every day? So, take guard to do battle with me.'
And, drawing his sword, he stood up facing the genie.

The genie was very pleased with Vikrama's heroism. 'O
king and great hero,' he said, ¡meeting a celestial personage
like me can never go waste. So ask me for any boon you
would like.' The king replied: 'If you are pleased with me,
then come whenever I think of you, and do my work for
me.' The genie agreed and went away. The next morning
Vikramaditya was appointed and crowned king with great
ceremony by his ministers.

IV. Vikrama and the Wicked Yogi

V ikramaditya ruled justly after becoming the king. He fulfilled the expectations of the gods and the priests, the orphans, the disabled and the afflicted. He took due care of the populace, satisfied his servants and retainers, and won the hearts of his nobles and ministers by keeping his promises. Thus did he reign happily.

Once a certain yogi came to the king, and said: 'Great hero, if you will not spurn my prayer, then I would like to ask you for a favour. For,

> Wealth, by its nature, is transient;
> so too is life, and even all existence.
> Then, why delay good deeds?'

'O yogi,' the king replied, 'if your work can be accomplished by me and what I possess, then you have but to ask.'

The yogi then said: 'King, the accomplishments of great men have always depended only on their natural prowess. For,

> Rāma had to conquer Lankā
> and to cross the ocean on foot.
> Rāvana opposed him on the battlefield,
> and his allies were only monkeys.
> Yet he slew the entire

race of demons in the war.[1]
The achievements of the great
flow from their inborn prowess,
not from any other devices.

'Majesty,' the yogi continued, 'I have undertaken to perform
an incantation ceremony. You must officiate in it as my
assistant.'

Vikrama agreed. The yogi then took him at night to a
forest. There he sent the king to fetch a corpse tied to the
branch of a tree, and himself commenced the ceremony
by reciting the incantation.

A genie had taken possession of the corpse. Knowing
that the king was in danger, it whiled away the night by
narrating twenty-five stories.[2] At dawn it appeared before
the king and said: 'Sire, this yogi is a sorcerer. You are the
best of men. He wishes to gain control of a golden being
by sacrificing you in his ceremony. Do not trust him. For,

One should never trust a rogue,
thinking that one has helped him.
The scoundrel and the snake
bite even those who feed them with milk.'

The king marvelled on hearing the genie. He said to
himself:

'The sins which fools commit for the sake of this life,
cause them sorrows in a thousand future lives.

'The wickedness! Well, be it so. What can he do? I too will
do whatever is needed. For,

The good man immersed in good deeds
lives in peace. The wicked one
with violent ways will writhe at his feet.

The snake drinks milk but brings forth
only venom. Yet an antidote will
make it as harmless as a lotús stalk.'

Reflecting on this, Vikrama took the initiative. He flung
the yogi into the sacrificial fire at the time of the final
oblation, and himself gained control of the golden being.
The latter's patron god then appeared and explained the
various powers which accompanied the being. He also
praised the king. The genie too was pleased with the king,
and promised him before leaving: 'Summon me in your
mind, and I will come to you like a slave. There is nothing
impossible for me, and I will do whatever you command.
The eight magic powers[3] will also be at your disposal.'

As for Vikramaditya, he took the golden being and
returned to his capital with all ceremony in the morning.

V. Vikrama gains the Throne

*T*here was no king on earth like Vikrama. His fame
spread throughout the three worlds, unimpeded like
the flow of the river Ganga. At this time the king of the
gods, Indra, wished to disturb the penances of the sage
Viśvāmitra. He summoned the nymphs Rambhā and Urvaśī
in heaven and said: 'Which of you two ladies is more
skilled in dance and music? Let her go to Viśvāmitra's
hermitage and disturb his penances. I will give her a prize
if she succeeds.'

'O king of the gods,' cried Rambhā, 'I am extremely
skilled in dance.' But Urvaśī said: 'Sire, I know how to
dance as prescribed in the sacred texts.' A dispute thus
having arisen between them, an assembly of the gods was
convened to take a decision.

Rambhā danced first. Urvaśī gave her performance on
the second day. All the gods were greatly pleased with
both. But they could not decide who was the better
dancer. Nārada the divine sage then spoke up. 'O king of
the gods,' he said, 'there is a monarch named Vikramaditya
on earth. He is an expert in all the arts, and specially so
in dance and music. He will be able to decide this dispute
between the two nymphs.'

Great Indra then sent his minister Mātali to Ujjayini to
fetch Vikramaditya. On receiving the invitation Vikrama
went with the genie to Amarāvatī, the celestial capital, and
saluted Indra who welcomed him with all honour.

Meanwhile a place for holding the dance competition had been readied. First Rambhā mounted the stage and gave her performance. On the following day Urvaśī took her place and danced in accordance with the sacred texts.

Vikramaditya praised Urvaśī and declared her to be the winner. 'How did you come to this conclusion?' Indra asked him. Vikrama replied: 'God, in dance the first and most important thing is bodily grace. This is stated in the Nritya Śāstra, the sacred text on this art[1].

The connoisseurs of dance say that grace
is more important than technique.
It lies in a fluent motion of the limbs,
moving neither too high or too low;
a symmetry of the hips and the knees,
the facial features and the ears;
a balanced raising of the breast;
and a sweet restfulness of the expression.

'Furthermore, the ballerina needs to demonstrate the particular posture appropriate to the beginning of a dance. The Nritya Śāstra specifies this as:

The limbs foursquare, the feet kept even,
and the hands held drooping like a vine:
this is the general rule for
the commencement of all dances.

'As for her appearance,

It should conform to the ideal
in the dancing master's mind.
The eyes should be large; the face,
radiant like the autumn moon;
the arms sloping from the shoulders;
the breasts small, firm and high;

the flanks smooth, as if polished;
a waist no more than a handspan;
a shapely bottom; and feet with curving toes.

'Specially charming is the moment of pause in a dance,

The left hand resting on the hip,
with a bracelet motionless on the wrist;
the other arm lying loose
like a young and slender bough;
the body's upper half held straight;
and the gaze dropped to the floor
where the toe plays with a flower:
the pause can be even more
delightful than the dance.

'In short,

Emotion is truly captured in dance
when the limbs convey fully
the meanings of the words within;
the feet identify with the moods
as they follow the rhythm
and the hands enact them delicately;
and the changing expressions of feeling
follow close on one another.

'That is why I applauded Urvaśī. She is a dancer as described in the Nritya Śāstra.'

The great Indra was satisfied. He honoured Vikramaditya with robes and presented to him a throne encrusted with rare and priceless gems. Thirty-two statuettes of precious moonstone supported this magnificent throne, which was mounted by stepping over their heads. 'From this royal seat,' the lord of heaven said to the king, 'may you protect the earth in all happiness for a thousand years.' And, taking the throne as decreed by Indra, Vikrama returned to his own capital, where he ascended it at an auspicious moment amidst the blessings of the priests, and ruled the earth unrivalled.

※

VI. Vikrama's Death and the hiding of the Throne

*V*ikramaditya's nemesis, Śālivāhana, was born many years later in the town of Pratishṭhāna,[1] fathered by the serpent king Śesha on a little girl. In Ujjayini the king and the people witnessed evil omens at the time, such as earthquakes, comets and fires on the horizon.

Vikrama summoned the soothsayers and asked them: 'Why do these omens occur day after day? What can they mean? Whose ruination do they portend?'

'Sire,' the soothsayers replied, 'the earthquake took place at dusk. This indicates evil for the king. As mentioned in the book of Nārada,

> An earthquake at dawn or dusk
> bodes ill for kings.
> And a yellow fire on the horizon
> is extremely unfavourable for them.

'In the book of Nārada it is further started,

> A comet is said to signal the destruction of kings.
> And a fire on the horizon,
> if it is yellow in colour,
> portends great danger for them.'

Vikramaditya then called his minister, Bhatti. 'Tell me,' he asked, 'what could these bad omens signify?'

'Who can say?' replied Bhatti. 'This looks to me like something unfavourable. What it is, only the future will show.'

'Why do you say unfavourable?' the king rejoined, 'I have nothing to fear. And listen to the reason, Bhatti. I will explain it all from the beginning.'

'In the past I had pleased the great god Maheśvara with my penances, and the dark-throated, three-eyed god had appeared before me. Filled with happiness, I bowed to him but forgot for a moment what else I should do. The god then told me to ask for what I desired.'

'I wanted immortality. So, I said to the god of gods: "Let the cause of my death be a son born to a two-and-a-half year old girl, and nothing else." The god confirmed this boon and returned to his abode on Mount Kailāsa. Since then I have always and everywhere been free from fear.'

After hearing this account the wise minister told the king: 'Well, everything is possible. Strange are the ways of our creator and saviour. He never has just one plan. King Hiraṇyakaśipu had been granted the boon that he could not be slain by any man or animal. Yet a youth who was neither one nor the other came into being to cause his death. Bearing this in mind, it would be better to mount a search for one who could pose danger for Your Majesty.'

'Very well,' said Vikramaditya, and he called in his mind for the genie who appeared instantly. Asked to hunt for a person such as the king had described, the genie bowed his head in acknowledgement of the great monarch's order, and sped forth through the sky, swifter than the wind.

After searching the seven continents, the seven mountain ranges and the seven oceans, the genie returned with his finding. 'I have looked at all that needed to be seen,' he reported, 'in the town of Pratishthāna, O King in the house of a potter, I saw a little boy like the newly risen sun. He was playing with a girl of hardly more than two and a half years. "Are you two related?" I asked. "This is my son," the little girl replied. "Who is your father?" I then asked, and she pointed to a brahmin who was there.

'I then questioned the brahmin. "This is my daughter," he said, "and that is her son." I was astonished. "How can this be?" I said to the brahmin. "The deeds of the gods are beyond our understanding," he told me. "The serpent king Śesha was charmed by her beauty and loveliness, and had intercourse with her. This child Śālivāhana was born as a result."'

Vikrama was amazed at the genie's report. He ordered his army against the town of Pratishṭhāna forthwith. But Bhatti, whose acumen was well known, said: 'Master, this is not the time for you to proceed against the enemy. It is better, sire, to follow the course of destiny from here itself.' The king accepted this advice and called off his preparations.

Later, at another time and for some other reason, the great king was impelled by fate to proceed with his army against Pratishṭhāna. When Śesha learnt that Vikramaditya was determined to kill his son, he too prepared an army to destroy the other force.

A battle took place between the two armies, and the forces of Śālivāhana prevailed over those of their opponent. Seeing his troops in retreat, Vikramaditya charged sword in hand to despatch Sālivāhana. But the boy saw him attacking, and struck him with a staff. The blow was like that from the staff of the god of death. Its force shook the king, who fell back quickly on Ujjayini. The protector of everyone returned like one who himself needs protection.

In Ujjayini Vikramaditya died, unable to bear the pain of his wound. All the king's wives prepared to enter his funeral fire. The ministers wondered what to do, for the king had no son. 'Let us find out if any of his wives is with child,' suggested Bhatti, and on investigation it was discovered that one was seven months pregnant. The ministers then got together and performed the coronation ceremony of the unborn child, and themselves undertook the management of the kingdom.

The throne presented by Indra stood vacant. One day a disembodied voice was heard in the assembly. 'O ministers of Vikramaditya, there is no more a king such as him, worthy of sitting upon this throne. Therefore let it be put away inside the earth at some good place.' The ministers thereafter buried the throne in a field of great purity.

*

VII. The Discovery of the Throne

*M*any years passed since the throne was hidden. Bhoja became the king. During his reign a brahmin once prepared a field where the throne had been interred, and planted it with sugarcane, chickpeas and suchlike. The field produced a rich crop and, to keep the birds away, the brahmin built a raised platform upon some high ground which also happened to be the spot where the throne was buried. There he would sit and drive off the birds.

Once King Bhoja passed by while out on a hunt with all the princes. The brahmin was on his platform. 'O King,' he called out, 'this field is in fruit. Come in with your warriors and eat whatever you like. Give the chickpeas to the horses. My life is today fulfilled, now that Your Majesty is my guest. When could I ever have had such an opportunity?'

The king and his party entered the field. The brahmin too came down from the platform to drive off some birds which had gathered in a corner. But he protested on seeing the king in the middle of the field: 'O King! What are you doing? This is not right! You are destroying this field, which belongs to a brahmin. If others commit an injustice, we appeal to you. If you yourself are set to act unjustly, who will stop that? It is said:

Who is there to control
a king turned libertine,
an elephant gone berserk,

and educated people
engaged in villainy?

'There is another thing. Your Majesty knows the law. How can you destroy the property of a brahmin? Such property is like poison, not to be touched. Thus,

> Poison is not as lethal, it is said,
> as the property of a brahmin
> which is the real poison.
> Taking the former kills only
> the individual, but the latter
> kills his children and grand-children too.'

On hearing these words the king and his entourage quit the field forthwith. At the same time the brahmin also returned to the platform after shooing off the birds. 'O King!' he called out again, 'why are you going away? This field is well ripened. Eat the sugarcane. The cucumbers are in fruit. Enjoy them!'

On the brahmin's pleas, the king once more returned to the field with his retinue. The brahmin too came down from the platform to chase the birds, and once again protested as before. 'How strange!' the king said to himself. 'When this brahmin mounts the platform, his mind is filled with generous thoughts. When he comes down he becomes mean-minded. Let me climb up and see for myself what this is.'

When King Bhoja ascended the platform, there arose within him an urge to free the whole world from its sufferings, to remove all people's poverty, to punish the wicked, promote the good and protect the populace in accordance with the law. He felt at that time prepared to sacrifice even his own life if it were needed. He was filled with a deep joy. 'What a wonderful field this is,' he reflected. 'It stimulates such thoughts by itself. It is said:

Some things have an innate tendency
to spread out by themselves:
like oil dropped on water;
a secret confided to a scoundrel;
a gift, however small, given
to the deserving; and learning
imparted to the intelligent.

'How can I ascertain the power of this field?' thought the king. He summoned the brahmin and asked: 'Brahmin, how much would you like for this field?'

'Master!' said the brahmin, 'you are skilled in everything. There is nothing you do not know. Do whatever is proper. The king is a veritable incarnation of the god Vishnu. On whomsoever his gaze descends, that person's miseries and afflictions are destroyed. The king is indeed a wish-fulfilling tree. Now that I have seen you, my misery and poverty are today at an end. As for this field, what does it matter?'

The king satisfied the brahmin with payments in cash and kind, and took possession of the field. He then ordered an excavation to be commenced beneath the platform. After a pit had been dug to the depth of a man's height, there came into view a beautiful single slab of stone. Under it there was a magnificent throne made of precious moonstones and studded with all kinds of gems. To it were joined thirty-two statuettes, each holding in its hands a jewelled lamp, as if for a ceremonial benediction. The extent of this great throne was thirty-two hands, and it was as high as an archer's bow.

Waves of bliss swept over King Bhoja's heart when he saw the throne. But when he tried to have it moved in order to take it to the city, it became heavier each time the porters attempted to lift it, and could not be budged at all.

'Why cannot this throne be moved?' the king asked his minister. 'Sire,' the latter replied, 'we do not know whose it is. But this throne is certainly unique and divine. It cannot be moved, nor can you gain it, without a fire sacrifice and other religious rituals.' The king then sent for the priests and had them perform all the ceremonies. After that the throne became light and movable by itself.

'At first I could not gain this throne,' the king told the minister. 'Thanks to your wisdom it has now come into my hands. This demonstrates how association with the wise can be a source of both pleasure and profit.'

'Listen, Your Majesty,' the minister replied, 'one who is himself wise, but does not pay heed to the wisdom of others, will always end in disaster. But you are not like that. You are wise, but still listen to good advice. That is why nothing can come in the way of all that you do.'

'The real minister is one who prevents harmful and accomplishes desirable ends,' observed the king. 'As it has been said,

> One whose counsel will resuscitate works
> which are stalled, consolidate those
> which are imminent, and eliminate
> those which can cause harm: such a person
> is indeed the best of ministers.'

'It is the duty of the minister to act for the benefit of his master, Your Majesty,' the minister responded. 'As it has been said,

> The real ministers of kings are they
> whose advice accords with the work required,
> and whose work accords with the master's benefit,
> not those who just blow their trumpets.

'Moreover, one should know that a state without a minister is useless—like a fort without provisions, good fortune without youth, renunciation without wisdom, peace with the wicked, good sense with hypocrites, love with harlots, friendship with scoundrels, the slave's independence, the poor man's rage, the servant's anger, the employer's cordiality, the beggar's home, the strumpet's devotion, honour among thieves and progress among fools.

'A king should honour the great, heed the wise, cherish gods and priests, and follow the path of justice. All these kingly virtues obtain in Your Majesty. You are best of kings. As for a minister, he too should have certain qualities, such as—a family tradition of holding office; familiarity with Kāmandaki,[1] Chāṇakya, the Panchatantra and other works on policy; and industry in the pursuit of his master's business. He should fear to sin, protect the populace and control the courtiers. Conformity with the king's inclinations; knowledge of what is proper for each occasion; and prevention of losses to the state are other ministerial virtues. A minister endowed with such attributes is worthy of holding office, just like the minister Bahuśruta, who saved king Nanda from committing the sin of a brahmin's murder.'

'How did that happen?' King Bhoja asked. 'Listen to the story,' said the minister.

*

VIII. The Minister's Tale

*I*n the city of Viśālā there once reigned a king named
Nanda. A mighty warrior, he had reduced all his rival
kings to vassalage by the force of arms, and ruled the land
as its sole sovereign lord. His son Jayapāla was versed in
the thirty-six weapons of war, and Bahuśruta was the name
of his minister.

The king's great love was his wife Bhānumati. He was
in fact infatuated with her, and spent all his time in her
company. Smitten by her beauty, he gave no thought to
state affairs. She would sit by his side even when he came
to the assembly. Once the minister said to him: 'Sire,

The king whose physician, preceptor, and minister
speak only sweet words will before long
lose his health, his morals, and his wealth.

'Therefore even the unpalatable needs to be said. Your
Majesty, it is not proper for the queen to come to the
assembly. Jurists and lawgivers have said that the royal
consort should not be exposed, even to the sun. But all
kinds of people can come here and look at her.'

'What you say is right, minister,' the king replied. 'But
what can I do? I cannot stay without her, even for a
moment.'

'Do this, then,' said the minister. 'Do what?' the king
interjected. 'Explain it.'

'Call a portrait painter,' said the minister, 'and have him make the likeness of Bhānumati on canvas. This can be hung on the wall before you so that you may look at her all the time.'

The king was impressed by this advice. He summoned an artist and told him to paint the portrait of Bhānumati. 'Sire,' said the artist, 'I must see her beauty with my own eyes before I can depict it limb for limb.' Bhānumati was then adorned and ornamented and displayed to the artist. He observed that she was a *padmini*, a lotus woman, and portrayed her with the features of this category. The attributes of the lotus woman are:[1]

She is delicate like the lotus bud;
her sexual fluid has the aroma
of a full blown lotus;
and a divine fragrance pervades
her limbs. Her eyes are
like that of a startled doe,
and tinged with red at the corners.
Her faultless pair of breasts
surpass the beauty of the bilva fruit.

Her nose is like the sesame blossom.
Her faith and devotion in the gods,
the elders and the brahmins
is constant. Fair as the champa flower,
she has the glow of a lily petal,
and her whole form, like the sheath
of a blooming lotus, covers
an inner incandescence.

The lotus woman is slender, and moves
gently and gracefully like the royal swan.
Her waist is adorned with a triple fold,
and her voice is sweet and swan-like.

She dresses neatly, and eats
gracefully, cleanly and daintily.
She is proud and very bashful,
and looks lovely in garments bright as flowers.

The painter depicted the queen accordingly, and submitted
the portrait to the king. The latter was delighted to see
his beloved thus portrayed, and ·rewarded the artist
appropriately. Thereafter the portrait of Bhānumati was
seen by Śāradā Nandana, the king's spiritual preceptor.
'You have delineated all the queen's features,' he told the
painter, 'but you have overlooked one.'

'Tell me, master,' the painter asked, 'what have I
overlooked?' Śāradā Nandana said: 'On her left hip there
is a mole like a sesame seed, which you have not portrayed.'

The king overheard what Śāradā Nandana had said.
To ascertain the reality, when he looked at Bhanumati's
left hip while they were making love, he observed that it
indeed bore a mole like a sesame seed. 'How could
Śāradā Nandana have seen this mole which is on a secret
part of her body?' he wondered. 'He has definitely had an
affair with her. Otherwise how could he know this? Besides,
with women such a situation is not to be doubted. Thus,

They jest with one, make eyes
at another, and think of someone else.
For women one man is never ·enough.

Fire is never sated with fuelwood,
the sea with the flow of rivers,
and death with living creatures;
nor are bright-eyed women ever sated with men.

There is no privacy, no opportunity, and no
man around as a suitor—thus alone, Nārada,
is the chastity of women assured.

The fool who is deluded enough
to think that a lovely woman is devoted
to him, merely passes into
her control to dance like a pet parrot.

One who acts according to women's words
or fancies, frivolous or even serious,
is bound to be looked down on in the world.

The man in love is squeezed by women
and trodden under foot like the seeds
of red lac, used for tinting the skin.'

Blinded by rage born of consternation, the king decided that the innocent Śāradā Nandana was guilty. Without further thought, he ordered Bahuśruta to put the brahmin to death. 'Great men of course are able to know everything,' the famous minister replied with all politeness, 'but one should not take decisions about believing this or that without thought. It is better to use one's discrimination and judgement.' The king's lip trembled at this response. 'If you wish me well,' he told the minister, 'just kill this villain.'

Commanded by the king, Bahuśruta had the brahmin Śāradā Nandana seized from his dwelling and publicly handcuffed. 'But what is his crime?' the minister worried. 'It will only harm the king's reputation if the preceptor is executed without reason. Who knows if his conduct was right or wrong, and how can anyone know? And why should the king be troubled for no cause? For the time being, therefore, I will continue to investigate this. In due course it will become clear if he is guilty or not.'

With these considerations in mind, Bahuśruta placed Śāradā Nandana in a dungeon and kept him concealed there. 'My lord,' he reported to the king, 'in accordance with your command, Your Majesty's instructions were carried out immediately.' As for King Nanda, he said nothing, and continued to repel his enemies and protect the kingdom.

IX. The Minister's Tale continued

After these events the king's son went out one day to hunt in the forest. There were bad portents at the time of his departure. Thus,

Rain out of season, then an earthquake;
similarly, a whirlwind and a shooting star:
such evil omens then occurred, and a friend
spoke out to avert the outcome.

It was the minister's son, Buddhisāgara, who spoke out on this occasion: 'Jayapāla, there is an extremely bad omen. Do not go out to hunt today.' But Jayapāla replied: 'Well, today we must test the validity of this bad omen.' 'Prince,' said his friend, 'wise people do not look for validity in omens of evil. It is said,

The wise man does not eat poison,
or play with snakes. Nor does he
disparage yogis or antagonize brahmins.'[1]

Though warned by his friend, the prince ignored his words and carried on. As he was leaving, Buddhisāgara once again said: 'Jayapāla, your end is near. Otherwise you would not be so perverse. As it is said,

No one ever made, or saw
or heard of a doe of gold.

Yet Rama thirsted to catch one.
When disaster strikes, the mind turns perverse.[2]

'But how can disaster occur except as a consequence of deeds earlier done? As it has been said,

There is no goodwill in harlots,
no permanence in wealth,
no discernment in fools,
and no getting away from
the consequences of one's actions.'

Meanwhile the prince had proceeded to the forest. After hunting down many animals, he saw a blackbuck antelope and followed it into a dense jungle. While he searched for it there, all his retinue turned back on their way home, and the antelope also disappeared.

Alone on horseback, Prince Jayapāla then saw a fine lake ahead. There he dismounted and tethered his horse to the branch of a tree. After a drink of water, at the very instant that he sat down under the tree's shade, there appeared a fierce tiger slowly emerging from the depths of a thicket. The prince's horse panicked. Swishing its tail and stamping the ground with its hooves, it broke the halter rope and fled. The prince too scrambled up the tall tree to save his life as the tiger, smelling a human, came forward quickly.

There was a bear sitting on the top branch of the tree. With a huge tiger at the bottom, the young prince was caught in the middle. Unable to climb up or to come down, or even to stay where he was, he lost his nerve in the crisis which had engulfed him. At that moment the bear spoke to him in a human voice: 'Prince, do not be afraid. I will protect Your Highness. Though I am only an animal, you should know that I follow the path of virtue.'

The prince was reassured. The bear asked him to come nearer, and, as he climbed up, it made room for him and seated him at its side. The tiger remained below, hoping to get at some meat. Meanwhile the sun set and it became dark.

At night, when the prince, who was very tired, began to feel sleepy, the bear addressed him again: 'Prince, you are about to fall asleep and will tumble down from the tree. So, come close to me and sleep in my lap.' And this is what the prince did.

The tiger now made friendly overtures to the bear. 'You and I are comrades,' said the tiger, 'we are permanent denizens of the forest. Keep our natural friendship in mind, and throw this human down. He will provide a full meal for both of us. Moreover humans are not to be trusted, specially if they are princes.'

'Whatever he may be,' the bear replied, 'he has taken refuge with me. I cannot throw him down. To cause the death of one who has sought sanctuary is a great sin. As it is said:

Those who betray a trust,
or a seeker of sanctuary
will live in a dreadful hell
till the final deluge.'

After some time the king's son woke up. 'Prince,' the bear said to him, 'I will sleep for a moment now. You remain alert.' The prince agreed, and the bear went to sleep near him. Then the tiger spoke again: 'Prince, do not trust this bear. He is a creature with claws. It is said,

One should not place one's trust
in creatures with claws or horns,
or in those who bear a weapon;
nor in rivers, women or royalty.

'Besides, he appears fickle minded. Therefore even his goodwill is to be feared.

'Pleased one instant, angry the next,
and dissatisfied
from moment
to moment—even the goodwill
of the capricious mind is to be feared.

'He wants to protect you from me, and to eat you himself.
So, on your part you should throw this bear down. I will
eat him and go away, and you too can go home.'

Jayapāla's suspicions were aroused by what the tiger
said. Thinking that the bear was asleep, the foolish young
man pushed the animal down. But the virtuous will never
perish, and even as it was falling, the bear hung on to
another branch. Once more the prince was terrified. 'You
sinner!' the bear cried, 'why are you quaking? Now you
must suffer the consequences of what you have done. You
will turn into a ghoul, and wander in the forest, babbling
the syllables 'sa, se, mi, ra'.

Morning came, and the tiger went away. The bear also
departed after cursing the king's son. And the prince became
a ghoul, wandering in the forest, and babbling 'sa, se, mi, ra'.

Frightened by the tiger, the prince's horse had run
back home. The king saw it and wondered what had
happened to his son. He proceeded to the forest with his
entourage to investigate and found the prince there, out
of his mind and muttering the sounds 'sa, se, mi, ra'. He
brought him home, but no antidote, including all kinds of
gemstones, incantations and herbs had any effect on his
son. 'If Śāradā Nandana had been here today,' the king
lamented, 'there would have been no need to worry about
my boy. But I myself had him done to death.' The minister
intervened at this point: 'Majesty, what is to be gained by
feeling sorry for what has already happened? Make a
proclamation with the beating of drums in the city, that if
anyone can restore the prince's health the king will give
him half his kingdom.'

Having had this done, the minister went home and narrated the whole story to Śāradā Nandana. The preceptor listened to the entire account and said: 'Minister, say this to the king: "I have a young girl whom the prince should see. She will be able to do something." Bahuśruta spoke accordingly to the king who then went to the minister's house with all his courtiers.

When the king was seated, with his son the ghoul by his side, muttering 'sa, se, mi, ra', Śāradā Nandana, who was hidden behind a curtain, recited four verses to release the prince from his affliction.

'Is there any cleverness in cheating
one's known well-wishers, and indeed,
is there any manliness in murdering
those who sleep in one's arms?'

On hearing this verse, which commenced with 'sa', the prince ceased mumbling that syllable, but continued to repeat the other three—'se, mi, ra'. 'How marvellous!' cried the delighted courtiers. The excellent brahmin then recited the second verse, which began with the syllable 'se':

'Even the slayer of a brahmin is released
from his sin when he beholds the bridge
across the sea at the point of Dhanushkoti,
but not the traitor to his friend.'

On hearing this stanza, Jayapāla dropped the second syllable also, and continued to mutter only 'mi, ra, mi, ra'. 'O what a great marvel!' the courtiers exclaimed, and Śāradā Nandana recited another verse full of faultless sense, beginning with the syllable 'mi':

'The traitor to his friend, the ingrate, the thief,
and one who violates the guru's bed—

all four will go to hell for as long
as the sun and the moon exist.'

The prince then let go yet another syllable and babbled
only 'ra, ra.' Once more the brahmin behind the curtain
recited in clear tones:

'King, if you desire your son's welfare,
give gifts to the deserving.
The householder is purified by charity.'

Even as Śāradā Nandana said this, the prince regained his
senses and became healthy. He recounted the story of the
bear to his father the king, who shook his head and stared
at the curtain in amazement. He went up to it all of a
sudden, his eyes wide with wonder, and asked:

'My good girl, you live in the village.
How did you know what happened
in the forest between
the bear, the tiger and this man?'

Once again there was the voice from behind the curtain:

'Listen carefully, O King!
Nothing is unknown to me.
By the grace of the god of gods,
Śāradā, the goddess of learning,
abides in my tongue. Through her
I know everything, just like
I knew of the mole on Bhānumati.'

The astonished king pulled the curtain aside, and beheld
Śāradā Nandana in person. He and all the others saluted
the brahmin, and the minister related all that had
transpired. The king then addressed the minister in front

of all the assemblage: 'Bahuśruta, I do not have even one benefactor to compare with you, sir. By your good sense you have averted a sin against the brahmins, and cured this prince who is so skilled in the ways of protecting this kingdom. Nothing can reciprocate your gift of his life. Through you I will now be able to conquer all the three worlds.

And honouring Śāradā Nandana the preceptor, and Bahuśruta the minister, King Nanda continued to rule the land with their guidance.

PART II

The Thirty-two Tales of the Throne

1. King Bhoja attempts to mount the Throne

*A*fter telling his tale to King Bhoja, the minister added: 'O King, the monarch who listens to his minister will have a long and happy life.' Bhoja praised the minister, and honoured him with robes, decorations and other gifts.

The king then proceeded to Dhārā, his capital, with the throne. He brought it into the city, and installed it at an auspicious moment in a thousand-pillared pavilion he had had erected. There he swiftly assembled all the things which are declared to be propitious for the consecration of kings: orpiment powder, turmeric, white mustard, sandalwood, flowers and sprouts of *dūrvā* grass, and other such articles. He had the earth with its seven continents depicted on a tiger skin, and a moon-white parasol put up before it with two fine jewelled maces and a pair of bright fly-whisks. Various kinds of swords and other weapons were placed on the side.

Brahmins versed in the four Vedas gathered from every side for the great occasion, as did the bards and the balladeers skilled in genealogy. Matrons who had living sons carried lamps in golden vessels for blessing Bhoja with lights. A variety of musical instruments were played repeatedly. All the citizens came dressed in their best for Bhoja's festival, and astrologers learned in the three branches of the science arrived to determine an auspicious moment for his enthronement.

Bhoja on his part was anointed and bathed without delay. He put on gleaming white garments and took a most beautiful sword in his hand. After meditating on his family gods and touching lucky objects, the king then went forth to mount the throne at the auspicious moment. A multitude of brahmins acclaimed him, and the bards sang his praises, as he awarded gifts and honours to all the four castes, and distributed various alms to the poor, the blind and the maimed. Escorted with the royal parasol and fly whisk, as he then placed his noble foot upon the head of the first statuette, she spoke to him in a human voice: 'O King! Do you possess valour, magnanimity, daring, nobility and other such qualities like *him?* If so, then mount this throne. Not otherwise!'

'O statue!' exclaimed the king, 'I too have magnanimity and all the other virtues of which you, speak. Which one do I lack? I too give whatever befits the occasion to all who come to me.'

'That itself is a shortcoming in you,' the statuette replied with a smile. 'What you have given, you proclaim with your own mouth. Only villains talk of their own virtues and the defects of others. The good never speak like that. It is said:

It is the wicked of this world
who talk of other's faults
as if they were their own virtues.
The good will never speak of others'
defects or their own merits.

'And further,

These nine should never be made public:
One's age, wealth, family secrets, magic spells,
medicaments, sexual liaisons, gifts,
and times of honour or disgrace.

'Therefore one should neither praise one's virtues or run down others. The mere mention of these cheapens a man.'

King Bhoja marvelled at the words of the statuette. 'What you say is true,' he said, 'one who makes much of his merits is no more than a fool. What I said was certainly inappropriate. But tell me now of the magnanimity of the man to whom this throne belonged.'

The statuette replied: 'O King, this is the throne of Vikramaditya. When he was satisfied he would give a million pieces of gold to supplicants:

One received a thousand pieces
of gold at a look from the king,
ten thousand at a word,
a hundred thousand when the king smiled,
and a million when he was satisfied.

'Such was the innate magnanimity of the emperor Vikramaditya. If you are capable of acting thus, then mount this throne.'

2. The Secret of the Sacrifice

When the time was ripe, King Bhoja once more came forward to mount the throne. The second statuette addressed him: 'King, you are worthy of sitting upon this throne only if you have the daring and the magnanimity of Vikramaditya.'

'What were those qualities like?' Bhoja asked. The statuette then told him in front of his assembled courtiers: 'King Vikramaditya unified the whole earth upto the ocean under his sovereign sway, and assured the welfare of all his subjects. Always eager to know what happened in the provinces, he never tired of being informed about everything by his confidential agents.

'Once a spy came to the king and acquainted him with all that he had seen. "Sire," he said, "on the mountain Chitrakūta there is a great shrine to the goddess and a famous prayer-grove with many trees. The grand temple there is built of priceless gemstones from Mount Mahāmeru. It rises high and shines like the goddess Bhavānī herself. On the mountain top there flows a stream of the river of paradise from whose waters can be known the sins and the merits of those who bathe in it. The drops which fall from the bodies of the virtuous are as white as milk; but the water becomes as black as soot when a wicked person enters it.

'"There is a brahmin engaged ceaselessly in a fire sacrifice on the mountain, since how long or for what reason, I do not know. He is there even now. The ash which has come out of his sacrificial fire pit is piled high like the peak of some huge hill. He observes some vow of silence and does not speak to anyone. Such, sire, is the sanctuary which I have seen on that mountain."

'"We would like to see this," the king told the spy. "Go on ahead, and the two of us will travel to where this noble brahmin is." He then proceeded swiftly with the spy to that holy mountain, and there saw the shrine, adorned with its great temple encircled by a four-gated rampart. The sanctuary would have purified even a sinner's heart, what to say of someone like the king whose inner self was delighted at being there. He bathed in the sacred stream which was shown to him by his man, and offered prayers to the great god *Śiva*. Thereafter he went to see the brahmin.

'At that time the brahmin was busy offering bilva fruit smeared with honey into the sacrificial fire. "Your Holiness," Vikramaditya asked him, "since how many years have you been conducting this fire sacrifice here? Do tell me all about it."

'"Listen, my good sir," the brahmin replied, "it is a hundred autumns since I have been here, performing this fire sacrifice with all the rituals and great effort. But my resolution to continue it till the fruit of the sacrifice is obtained has been futile. The goddess just will not grant her grace."

'After listening to the brahmin the king, with all solemnity, himself offered a bilva fruit smeared with honey as an oblation into the sacrificial fire. Observing that the goddess was still not propitiated, he then decided that his own head must be sacrificed. As he put his scimitar to his throat and was about to make the incision, the goddess appeared and herself restrained his hand. "My son, I wish you well," she said, "do not act in haste. Choose a boon, for I grant wishes. I have come, and I will give you whatever you desire, no matter how hard it may be to get."

'Commanded thus, the king replied with all reverence: "Goddess, I would like to know why you have not granted your grace to this brahmin who has been sacrificing to you with so much effort since such a long time, while you have favoured me within moments of seeing me."

'The goddess was precise. "You are zealous and prepared to take risks for dharma," she said. "Listen carefully to the reason. Even though he sacrifices to me, his mind is not fixed on me in devotion. That is why he does not succeed. As it is said of praying with the rosary:

> When beads are told only with the fingertips,
> when they are told unmindful of the round
> completed, and when they are told
> with thoughts somewhere else:
> in all these the effort is fruitless.

'"You see, this brahmin's heart lacks devotion:

> God does not dwell in wood or stone
> or mud, but in pure devotion
> from which all else proceeds."

'After listening to these words of the deity, the king responded: "Goddess, the world should know of the fruit of your grace. You had earlier asked me to choose a boon, and gods certainly never contradict themselves:

> Kings give their word but once,
> and so do the gods. Only once
> is a virgin offered in marriage.
> All these three do not happen again.

'"Therefore, goddess, give me this boon which I seek. Let the desires of this long suffering brahmin be satisfied."

'"So be it," said the goddess, and giving the brahmin whatever he wanted, she disappeared forthwith. The brahmin too went home, fully contented. And King Vikramaditya returned to his capital.

'King Bhoja,' the statuette concluded, 'if you too possess such daring and magnanimity, then sit upon this throne.'

3. The Four Jewels

*A*s King Bhoja was once again about to sit upon the throne, another statuette addressed him: 'O King, this seat may be occupied only by one who has the magnanimity of Vikrama.' 'Tell me a tale of his magnanimity, statue,' requested Bhoja.

'Listen, O King,' said the statuette, 'there has never been a ruler like Vikramaditya on this earth. In his thinking there was no differentiation between compatriots and outsiders: he provided for the welfare of everyone. It is said,

It is the small-minded who
differentiate between 'us' and 'them'.
For the large hearted the world itself is one family.[1]

'Moreover, no one has had his daring, industry and steadfastness. Indra and the other gods used to assist him. It is said,

Even the gods are wary of one
in whom the six qualities
of daring and steadfastness, industry and intelligence,
and strength and valour are combined.

'Furthermore, O King, God in turn accomplishes the wishes of those who fulfill the longings of their supplicants. As it is said,

God fulfills the wishes
of men with a firm resolve,
as did Vishnu with his discus and eagle
for the weaver in the battle.'

'How was that?' asked Bhoja and the statuette recounted a marvellous tale, delighting the hearts of all the assembled courtiers.

Vishnu and the Weaver

There is a city called Pratāpa-Vishama in the Vindhya mountains. In it there ruled King Brihatsena, who had a daughter named Sulochanā. A rogue of a weaver was infatuated with this princess, and used to wonder how he could have her, bearing in mind that she stayed within the palace.'

'Some resourceful person soon devised for the weaver an eagle and a discus similar to what the god Vishnu has. These were made of wood and worked with a cord. Using them, the rogue flew up to the palace and approached Sulochanā of the bewitching smile. "Know that I am Vishnu, my beauty," he told her. "I have come here just for your sake." Having seduced the girl with such words, he would come flying every day and enjoy her at leisure. This continued for a long while with the concurrence of Brihatsena, who too was enticed into believing that the weaver was the god Vishnu.'

'Considering that a god had become his son-in-law, the king now entered into confrontations with many other powerful rulers. Afraid of Vishnu, they put up with his provocations at first; but eventually all of them got together and consulted each other: "Brihatsena is a wicked man. Now that Vishnu has become his son-in-law, the villain does not only want tribute, even though it is offered willingly, but is after our very lives. It is better now to fight him, even if we die." Taking this decision they suddenly besieged his capital in force.

'Full of arrogance, Brihatsena came out boldly from his fortress and battled on his own against his many opponents with their numerous forces. But when his soldiers had been killed by their warriors and he himself had been wounded, he had to beat a painful retreat back into the city where he acquainted his daughter with his discomfiture. She on her part went in anguish to her spouse and entreated him. "You my husband are Vishnu," the simple girl said to the rogue, falling at his feet, "now save my father from this plight."

'The weaver could think of no way out and prepared himself for his own end. He picked up his wooden discus, mounted his mechanical bird and, grasping its pulley, flew out into the air, shouting "Run away! Run away! I am Vishnu!"

'The opposing hosts got ready for battle. In that moment Vishnu, the lord of the world who sleeps on the serpent, reflected: "This man has put on my guise and declared himself to be Vishnu. If he is slain by his opponents my reputation will be jeopardized!" Thinking thus, the discus-wielding lord promptly went forth on his eagle and scattered the enemy forces, before returning to his own seat.

'Observing the enemy's unexpected rout, the rogue duly returned and announced a victory to his father-in-law. This shows how, when someone resolves firmly to do something, the gods themselves come to his aid. This is even more so in the case of a righteous person.'

'If a man is energetic and prompt,
knows his work and is free of vices,
and has courage, gratitude and firmness
of purpose, the goddess of prosperity
will herself seek him out
to be her dwelling place.

'Thus was King Vikramaditya, an abode of all the virtues and possessed of every excellence. Once he said to himself: "Oh, this world is transitory! No one can know what will happen, when and to whom. Therefore, the wealth that one accumulates is useless unless it is spent in enjoyment or given away in charity. The best use of money is in fact in charity to the deserving. Otherwise it only goes waste. It is said:

> There are three courses for money:
> charity, enjoyment and going waste.
> For one who neither gives
> nor spends, there remains
> only the third option.

And further:

> Wealth should either be enjoyed
> or given away, but never hoarded.
> Look at how the honey collected
> by bees is taken away by others.

> Enjoy your money and give it away.
> Honour the honourable and revere
> the good. Wealth is as transient
> as a lamp's flame flickering in a gusty wind."

'Thinking thus, the king organized a religious festival for charity. In it honours were accorded to all those deemed worthy on account of their knowledge, deeds, asceticism or artistic skills. Gifts were given to the poor, the weak and the helpless, in keeping with their requests. The eighteen classes of subjects were exempted from tax. Worship with all the ritual of invocations, vows and sacrifices was offered to the divinities of the celestial and the nether regions, of land and water, of cities and villages; and to the guardian deities of the fields, the directions and the quarters. The king's own emissaries were sent everywhere to invoke the attendance of all the gods on this occasion.

'A certain brahmin was sent by the king to invite the Ocean. He went to the seashore and, having made the sixteen ritual offerings with flowers, fragrances and other things, cried out: "O Ocean, King Vikramaditya will be performing a sacrifice. At his direction I have come here to invite you to attend it." With these words he placed a handful of flowers in the water and remained standing there for a while.

'But there was no response to his words. The brahmin was disgusted. "Who else would have been mad or unlucky enough to get sent on an errand such as this?" he said to himself, "Whom have I come here to invite, and who will give me an answer? Whoever spoke to the waters and received a reply?

> Where there are no greetings,
> no kind words, no talk even
> of faults and merits:
> one would be a fool
> ever to go to such a place,
> even if it were heaven.

'"Well, I was commanded by the king and I have done my duty," the brahmin said aloud as he turned back, dejected. But, as he was returning to his village, someone with a shining visage and a priestly garb came up to him and said: "You, O brahmin, were sent by Vikrama to invite us. We acknowledge this honour. Gifts and honours at the appropriate time are indeed the signs of a friend. It is said:

> These six are the signs of friendship:
> to give and to receive gifts;
> to tell and to ask secrets;
> and to entertain and be entertained.

'"Furthermore, one should not think that friendship is destroyed by distance and flourishes only in propinquity. What upholds it is affection. It is said,

One who abides in your heart
is close to you, even though he
be far away. But one who is distant
from your mind is far indeed
even though he stand nearby.

And further:

The cloud in the sky and the peacock
on the hill; the sun in the heavens
and the lotus in the pool;
the moon at double that distance
and the lily on earth:
one's friend is never far from one.

'"Therefore I will certainly come. But I too have an errand for you. I wish to present to the king these four priceless jewels which you should give to our dear Vikrama. Their powers are as follows: the first produces gold, day and night; from the second comes an army with its four divisions to vanquish all enemies; the third provides food cooked in different flavours; and the fourth gives as much precious clothing and jewellery as one may desire. Take these jewels given by the Ocean with all affection, and hand them over to the king."

'The brahmin took the jewels and returned to Ujjayini. Much time had passed meanwhile. The sacrificial ceremony was over, the king had completed the final ablutions and sated the people with his bounty. The brahmin met him, submitted the jewels, and explained the powers of each one. "Your Reverence," said the king, "you have come at a time when the distribution of the sacrificial fees is already over. I have paid their fees to all the brahmins. You may now take one of these four jewels. Choose whichever one you like."

'"Your Majesty," replied the brahmin, "I will go home

and ask my wife, son and daughter-in-law. I would like to take the jewel which pleases them all." The king agreed.

'The brahmin then went home and explained the situation to his family. "The most desirable of these is the jewel which produces an army," said his son, "with that we can easily gain a kingdom." "You prefer kingship," the father retorted, "but everything flows from gold. So, we should take the one which gives out gold." But the wife told them both: "What will one do with a kingdom or with wealth? Man's life depends on food. The jewel which will provide meals is the best." The daughter-in-law however insisted: "Let it be the one which gives as many garments and jewelled ornaments as one wants. The rest are all of no use." Arguing thus with each other, they all got into a quarrel.

'Sick at heart, the brahmin went back to the king. He returned all the jewels to him and told him about the conflicting demands of his family members. The king was gracious. To satisfy them all, he presented the entire set of the four jewels to the brahmin who went home overjoyed.'

Concluding the tale, the statuette said: 'O King, magnanimity is a spontaneous quality, not something put on. Thus,

Like fragrance in champaka blossoms
radiance in pearls, and sweetness
in the sugar cane, magnanimity
is something innate.

'If you possess such magnanimity, only then may you sit on this throne.'

4. A Test of Gratitude

*O*n another occasion, as King Bhoja was again about to mount the throne after having made all the arrangements for his coronation ceremony, the fourth statuette spoke to him: 'O King, only one who has Vikramaditya's sense of gratitude for favours received may sit upon this throne. Mount it if you can repay a good turn like him.'

'What was his gratitude like?' the king asked. 'Listen, Your Majesty,' replied the statuette, 'there was an eminent man of learning in the city of Ujjayini. His virtuous wife was very unhappy as she had no son. "Lord, you have the insight of wisdom, and know every thing," she asked her husband humbly, her hands clasped together, "tell me why I do not have a son."

'"Listen, my dear," the brahmin replied to his wife, "I will tell you if there is faith in your heart. An intelligent person can earn wealth with due effort, but fame and progeny are two things which cannot be obtained on this earth except by propitiating the great god Śiva."

'The pious lady then told her husband: "If what we desire can be attained by praying to the great god, let us then worship that lord with all ceremony, so that with his grace a good son may be born to me."

'The brahmin commenced the worship of Śiva in keeping with his wife's counsel. Wise people do not neglect advice just because it is given by a woman. Besides, he had heard the ancient saying:

One should not take poison from
someone merely because he is learned,
nor bad advice because he is full of years;
but nectar should be accepted even from
a yokel, and good words even from a child.

'After the brahmin and his wife had begun praying to
Śiva together with his consort Pārvatī and son Skanda,
the great god appeared to him in a dream and told him
that he would obtain a male offspring when he had
observed a ritual fast on a Saturday which was also the
thirteenth day of the lunar month. Thus commanded by
the god, the brahmin undertook the fast in the prescribed
manner, and happily became in consequence the father of
a son.

'The brahmin performed his son's birth ceremony,
and named him Deva Datta on the twelfth day. He followed
up with all the other important rites, from the first feeding
with rice to the investiture with the sacred thread, after
which he instructed his son in the scriptures, the law
books and all the arts. In the boy's sixteenth year the
brahmin held his tonsure ceremony, and then got him
married and settled in a livelihood. Himself wishing to set
out on pilgrimage, he finally offered the lad his parting
counsel: "Pay heed, my son. I am giving you this advice for
your welfare in this and the next world. Never forsake your
duties even if you are in extreme difficulties. Never argue
with strangers. Have compassion for all creatures. Be
devoted to the great god. Do not covet other men's wives.
Do not quarrel with the powerful. Follow the wise. Suit
your words to the occasion, and your expenses to your
means. Good people should be cultivated and the wicked
avoided. Do not tell secrets to women."

'Having exhorted his son repeatedly in this manner
about proper conduct, the brahmin went away with his
wife to Vārānasī. And Deva Datta remained in the city,
following his father's advice.

'Once Deva Datta was cutting wood in the hillside
forest for a fire sacrifice. King Vikramaditya, wishing to
hunt, went with his men to the forest at the same time.
There he came upon a mighty boar and chased it all alone
on horseback, his bow uplifted to shoot. Pursuing it from

glade to glade, he brought down the great beast, but in the process was separated from his retinue and lost his way.

'Seeing Deva Datta with his load of firewood, the king asked the brahmin how to get to the city. The latter not only pointed out the way, but also offered fruit and water to the king, and accompanied him to the capital, himself marching ahead.

'A long time passed. Once the king mentioned in court the good turn the brahmin had done him. "How can I repay my debt to Deva Datta?" the king said. "He brought me to the city from the depth of a great forest." Someone remarked on this occasion: "How good is this man! He does not forget any favour done to him. As it is said,

> Remembering the little bit of water
> it was nourished with in its youth,
> the coconut tree bears a load
> of fruit upon its head and gives
> a nectar-like juice to men
> as long as it lives: the good
> never forget the favours they receive."

'The brahmin heard about the king's statement. "The king speaks thus," he said to himself, "but is it true or false? The reality has to be seen." He then somehow hid the king's son in his own house without anyone knowing it, and sent a servant with one of the prince's ornaments for sale in the city.

'Meanwhile a tremendous commotion had broken out in the royal palace that the prince had been murdered by some thief, and the king himself had despatched his officers to search everywhere for his son. When they looked in the market place, the found Deva Datta's servant there with an ornament in his hand. Recognizing it to be the prince's, they tied him up and took him to the king. "You villain!" they questioned him "How has this ornament

come into your possession?" "It was given to me by Deva
Datta the brahmin," the man replied. "I am his servant. He
sent me to the market to sell the ornament and bring back
the money."

'The king swiftly summoned Deva Datta, and enquired
about all that had happened. The brahmin hung his
head as if in fear. While the people mostly took him to
be the culprit, he just stood in the court and said nothing
for a while. Then he spoke haltingly: "I abducted and
killed your son for the sake of money. Sentence me as
such."

'When they heard this, the courtiers who were present
cried out: "Cut this villain into nine pieces! Grind him in
an oil mill! Bind him with ropes of grass, and burn him on
the highway! Whatever the method, he deserves to be put
to death by torture."

'The king did not approve what the courtiers said. He
remembered the good turn done to him in the past, and
himself addressed Deva Datta: "Sir, you took care to show
me the way when I was alone in the forest, and saved my
life. But for that where would my kingdom be, and where
indeed my progeny? This pardon will be some recompense,
but I will still remain indebted to you. Have no fear that
it will be otherwise." With these words, that forgiving
monarch praised Deva Datta and dismissed him with
decorations and robes of honour.

'The brahmin brought back the prince and restored
him to his father. The king was astonished. "O Deva
Datta!" he exclaimed, "why did you do all this?" "Listen,
Your Majesty," replied the brahmin. "You often asked in
the assembly: 'How can I ever repay my debt of gratitude
to Deva Datta?' So, I did this to test your heart. The result
is revealed in yourself."

'"One who forgets an act of kindness is the basest of
men," the king commented. But Deva Datta said: "Your
Majesty is kind to the whole world, even without any

ulterior motive. That is why you are the best of all the people. As it is said,

> Those who live to do good
> to others, even without reason
> they indeed are the best, the blessed
> adepts of virtue at all time."

'The courtiers too cried out in amazement:

> "The earth upholds these two
> or, it may be said, these two
> uphold the earth:
> one whose heart
> is engrossed in doing kindness; and one
> who never forgets a kindness done."

'Thus, O King,' concluded the statuette, 'if you are possessed of such a sense of gratitude, then sit with ease upon this throne.'

5. A Dilemma of Duties

*W*hen the lord of the Bhojas once more proceeded to mount the throne, he came to the fifth statuette. 'A man of such magnanimity and depth of character is alone worthy of sitting upon this throne,' she said, addressing the king. 'Listen, a certain great merchant once brought some gemstones and showed them to the emperor Vikramaditya. After he had sold them to the monarch at an appropriate price, the merchant exhibited yet another gem to him. The roseate glow of this precious jewel left the assembly stock still with amazement never seen before. Vikrama specially praised and commended the merchant, asking him if he had another similar gem. "There are ten others finer than this one, O king of kings," said the merchant, "they are at my village. Send someone for them if you like."

'The king was pleased to hear this. With the help of his own men of affairs he appraised the ten gems at ten millions each. He then asked a retainer to go and fetch them. "We must see you without fail on the eighth day from today," he told the officer, who bowed his head in acknowledgement of this difficult order, and set off immediately.

'On the eighth day the officer returned to the city with the gems, but presented only five before the king. "Where are the other five?" Vikrama asked him. The officer clasped his hands together and said humbly: "Sire, as commanded by you I obtained the ten gems immediately, but halfway on my journey back I was overtaken by rain. My path was blocked by a raging river, its waters muddied and its banks overflowing in a flood. I was greatly worried. The river was difficult to ford. There was no one to take me across. How was I to get back that very day? Luckily for me a man came by. 'Friend, will you take me across this river?' I asked. 'Traveller,' he said to me, 'this river is overflowing its banks today. How can it be forded? Moreover, a wise man should avoid crossing a river in flood. As it is said,

> Fording a flooded river,
> quarrelling with a powerful man,
> and confronting a numerous crowd,
> are things to be eschewed from afar.

Similarly,

> Never put your trust
> in the deeds of women,
> the favour of kings,
> the friendship of serpents,
> the affection of businessmen,
> and the fording of swollen rivers.'

"'What you say is true enough, ferryman,' I replied, 'but I have important work to do. And what needs to be done specially has priority over what is generally done. As it is said,

> The exception indeed prevails
> over the general rule;
> or, as one may see, the first
> generally supercedes the second.

"'Thus, crossing the river is a general matter for me, but the king's business must prevail over it. Even what you say is of no consequence in comparison to the importance of such work. I have to be present today itself at the royal feet, and which man can dare to transgress the king's command?'

"'When I spoke like this, the man looked at me and said: 'I will take you across the river if you give me five of the gems.'

'"A great debate then ensued within my mind. Should I give such a fording fee, or should I not? If I give away the king's property it will spoil the reputation of my judgement. If I do not, I will be in the great danger of disobeying the king's command. What could be the way out in these circumstances, which I might follow for my safety?

'"While I was in this dilemma, a great thought came to my mind. Lovely garments, bright and soft; abundant wealth; ornaments radiant with splendid gems; beautiful women of extraordinary charm and virtue: all these are commonplace for the very affluent, and result moreover, merely in material enjoyment. What is particular for kings is that their orders are carried out on this earth.

'"With this thought, two ancient stanzas passed through my memory:

The object of asceticism is chastity;
of learning, full knowledge;
of wealth, charity and enjoyment;
and of authority the only
object is to be obeyed.

To disobey kings, to dishonour
the learned, and to consign
women to a separate bed,
is said to be the same
as killing them without a weapon.

"Arriving at this conclusion, and afraid of disobeying your commandment, I gave away five of the gems to cross the river and come to your feet."

'King Vikramaditya was pleased to hear his servant's statement,' said the statuette, 'and gave him the remaining five gems as an appropriate reward. If such magnanimity and sense of propriety obtains in Your Majesty, then, Great King, mount this mighty throne.'

6. Distress and Deceit

*W*hen King Bhoja had once again found an auspicious day and wished to mount the throne, another statuette spoke to him: 'King, only when you become as great in munificence as Vikramaditya will Your Majesty be worthy of mounting this throne.' 'Tell me,' asked the king, 'what was his munificence like?'

'Once the noble King Vikrama was in his assembly hall in the capital of Avanti,' said the statuette. 'It was spring. The keeper of the parks and the gardens was announced in by the ushers. Saluting with folded hands raised to the forehead, he said: "Sire, the trees and the plants in your pleasure park are full of new shoots, flowers and fruit, specially the mangoes, coconuts, citrons, custard apples, oranges, nutmegs, frangipanis, asokas, palms, acacias, plantains, kankoli berries, cloves, screwpines, jasmines and the lavali creeper. It is now the time of the spring festival." Hearing this, the king proceeded to the pleasure park, accompanied by his chief queen, concubines, dancing girls and others.

'There, Vikramaditya entered a vast inner quarter to amuse himself. It was like the abode of Indra, the king of heaven. It shone with tall arches and pillars of gold, ruby columns, moonstone balconies and stairways of sapphire. A garden bloomed there, splendid with mango, frangipani and asoka trees, and resonant with the warblings of nightingales. Its ornamental pools gleamed with steps of turquoise, their water flecked with pollen scattered by the blossoming lotus. The garden was provided with playhouses, their roofs well covered with sand, and their walls with fragrant grass and other creepers to keep the interiors cool.

'The place was aglitter with courtesans in sparkling jewellery. They were of all the four sorts, the young and the mature, the artless and the bold. Some wore rich saffron robes, some garments white as milk, and some costumes as colourful as painted pictures. Among them were women skilled in witty conversation, puns, allusions and persiflage; and expert in the bodily language of dance and mirth, coquetry and affection, allurement and passion. These beauties included the four categories[1] of *padmini* or the lotus woman, *hastini* or the elephant woman, *śankhini* or the seashell woman, and *chitrini* or the picture woman. With them the king gathered flowers, dallied in the water, made music, sported on the swings, and played woman's house and other games. He enjoyed there the most exquisite delights of this earthly existence. He was like an elephant with his mates or like someone in a play with no other man in the cast.

'Near the park was a shrine of the goddess Chandikā, and a celibate lived there. "Alas, I am wasting my life in penances," he said to himself as he saw the king arrive. "I have never experienced any pleasures, even in a dream. What kind of reasoning is it that one should suffer as long as one lives, so that the fruits of penance may be tasted after one is dead? Some people say that it is wise to eschew physical pleasures as they are intertwined with pain. But these are foolish thoughts. It is said:

> It is a foolish idea that men should
> renounce the pleasures of the senses
> because they are accompanied by pain.
> What man with self-interest would ever
> throw away rice rich in fine white grains
> just because it is mixed with a few bits of their husk?[2]

'"Therefore, even at the risk of great pain, one should definitely savour the pleasure which is woman. It is the best thing in this worldly round. It is said,

> A gazelle-eyed girl is the best thing
> in this worthless worldly round.

For her sake men seek wealth.
Without her what is the point of having it?

A lovely woman is the best thing
in this worthless worldly round.
It is with this thought in mind
that the great god gave her half his body.

'"Now that King Vikramaditya has come here," the celibate
thought, "I will therefore beg him for a grant of land so
that I may marry some girl and partake of earthly pleasures."
He then went to the king, sat down at his bidding, and
offered him his best blessings.

'"From where have you come, brahmin?" the king
asked. "I stay here itself, serving the mother of the world,"
the man replied, "I have spent fifty years, serving her all
the time. I am a celibate. The goddess came to me in a
dream today as night was ending, and said: 'O brahmin, I
am pleased with you, who have undergone hardship for so
long in serving me. Now you must accept to become a
householder, and beget a son, before applying your mind to
salvation. Otherwise you cannot attain that end. It is said,

One may apply the mind to salvation
after one has discharged the three debts.[3]
One who seeks salvation without
discharging them will go to hell.

'"Thus,' said the goddess, 'having been a celibate, one
should become a householder; having been a householder
one should become a forest dweller; and having been a
forest dweller one may enter into the life of a wandering
sanyasi. Moreover I have appeared to King Vikrama in a
dream and spoken to him. He will fulfill your wishes.' This
is what the goddess said to me in a dream, and so I have
come to you."

'When the celibate spoke these deceitful words to the king, the latter said to himself: "The goddess told me nothing in a dream. This man is lying, and so be it. Nevertheless, he seems to be in distress, and there is no question that his wish should be fulfilled. It is said,

> Thirsty peacocks cry out in distress
> to the rainclouds, and the clouds
> instantly pour down streams of water for them.
> What is the cloud to the bird,
> or the bird to the cloud? Those who
> are in distress should not
> fail to ask, and those who are
> great-hearted should not fail to give."

'The king then had a new city built for the brahmin, appointed him as its ruler, and presented him with a hundred slave girls, before returning to his own capital. And the brahmin, his wishes all fulfilled, continued to pray for the king's prosperity.'

After recounting this tale, the statuette said to King Bhoja: 'Your Majesty, sit on this throne if you are possessed of such munificence.' But the king was silent.

7. The Decapitated Duo

*T*he seventh statuette stopped the king with charming words when, seeing that the day was auspicious, he wished once again to mount the throne. 'Why do you stop me?' he asked. 'Listen, great king,' the statuette replied, 'the reason why I stop you is the mighty deeds of Vikramaditya.'

'The noble Vikrama was king in Avanti. Under his rule, the people eschewed the seven vices. Nor did they transgress the rules of their respective castes. They deliberated on the scriptures and pondered on the ultimate reality. Delighting in virtue, they feared to sin, sought renown, and made a habit of helping others. Truthful in speech, uninterested in acquisition, silent in slandering others, they meditated on the supreme soul and despised the physical body. They had goodness in their hearts and the generosity which comes from knowing that wealth is transitory.

'A merchant named Dhanada lived in Avanti at that time. He was so rich that he did not know the extent of his own wealth. Whatever goods were to be seen in the city could be obtained in his house. "I have acquired everything in this world," he once said to himself, "but nothing at all for the next. Without that all is fruitless here. For,

What is the use of acquiring riches sufficient
to satisfy all one's desires; of bringing
all one's enemies underfoot; and of
preserving this human body for an age;
if the soul is not devoted
to the practice of righteousness?"

'So Dhanada performed meritorious charities as prescribed in the Book of Gifts[1] at his home, and proceeded abroad on pilgrimage to holy places. On the way he took a ship and went to an island in the ocean. There he saw a shrine to the goddess behind a lake enclosed with moonstone slabs. On the left of the shrine were to be seen a beautiful couple, a man and a woman, their heads separated from their bodies. This had been devised by the goddess to test virtuous people. A stone inscription was on view there: "These two will come to life whenever some hero offers his own head here as a sacrifice."

'The great merchant was amazed to see this decapitated duo next to the temple. His limbs broke out in perspiration and his hair stood on end, as he blinked and trembled, his mind in a whirl. Somehow controlling himself, that wise man came out of the shrine and returned to where he was staying.

'After completing his pilgrimage Dhanada returned home. He presented holy souvenirs to his relatives and, taking something precious, went the next morning to see the king. It is said,

> One should never go empty-handed to a king,
> to a temple, a guru and, specially, to an astrologer.
> With a gift one can indicate another
> to be expected in return.

'And similarly,

> One should never go empty-handed
> to a beloved wife, a dear friend,
> a young son, an astrologer, and the king.

'After Dhanada had presented his gift and taken a seat, the king asked if his journey had gone well, and enquired about anything unusual that may have happened. Dhanada told him about the shrine of the goddess in the middle of the ocean.

'The king too was amazed. "Come with me, Dhanada," he said, "we both will go there and see this marvel." He then went with the merchant by sea to the island, and saw the couple, man and woman, and read the inscription.

'The king's mind was filled with compassion. He told himself:

'If a man can help others,
but does not do so, this error
will lose him his own soul
which he may have earlier gained."

'After performing his ablutions and ritual donations, as he then raised a sword to his throat, and was about to cut off his own head, the goddess restrained his hand. "O man of virtue," she said, "I am pleased with you. Ask for a boon." "If you are pleased with me," replied the king, "bring these two to life and grant them a kingdom." "O virtuous man, this arrangement was made as a test," the goddess said further. "You alone are the ornament of this world. No one else is as virtuous as you." Thereafter the king returned to his capital.'

After telling this tale, the statuette said to King Bhoja: 'If you have such daring, then mount upon this throne.'

8. The Filling of the Lake

*W*hen King Bhoja approached the throne once again in order to mount it, the eighth statuette addressed him: 'O King, you may mount this throne only when you have an abundance of heroic daring like Vikramaditya.' At these words the king's mind was filled with curiosity. He asked about this heroism, and the statuette replied: 'Through his spies King Vikrama would learn all about various interesting and wonderful incidents and other marvellous accounts from all over the world. It is said:

> Cattle perceive through their sense of smell,
> brahmins through the scriptures,
> and kings through their spies;
> other people perceive merely
> through their two eyes.

'Listen, Your Majesty, when one is a king, it becomes necessary to know fully the condition of the people and the mood prevailing everywhere. The people should be nurtured, the wicked punished, and the good protected. The collection of revenue should be just, and the treatment of petitioners equal. These indeed are five sacred rites for kings. As it is said:

> Punishing the wicked;
> honouring the good;
> augmenting the treasury justly;
> impartiality among petitioners;
> and protection of the realm:
> these five are called
> the king's acts of worship.

'And further,

What use are prayers by a king
who oppresses his subjects? His prayers,
rosaries and fire sacrifices consist in ensuring
that no tears are shed in the country.

'When Vikrama ruled thus, two of his spies once returned to the royal presence after having travelled round the world. Questioned by the king, they said: "Your Majesty, there is a certain very wealthy merchant in the land of Kashmir. He had a reservoir for water dug with an extent of ten miles, and a temple to the god Nārāyaṇa the Waterborne erected in the middle. But water does not stay in this tank. The merchant had brahmins perform a fourfold sacrifice to the water god Varuna with libations and the rest in order to get the tank filled; but even then the water would not stay.

'"The merchant was dejected. He would sit every day on the side of the tank, heaving sighs: 'Alas, the water does not stay here. No method works at all. All this labour has been in vain.' Once, while he was sitting thus, a supernatural voice was heard from the sky: 'What is this, merchant's son? Why do you heave sighs? This tank will have clear water only when it is sprinkled with blood from the neck of a man with the thirty-two auspicious marks, and not otherwise.'

'"On hearing these words, the merchant immediately applied his mind and thought of a method for accomplishing what he wanted. He had statues made with seven million pieces of gold as the price of blood from the neck of a man bearing the thirty-two marks, and got them set up by the side of the tank with a verse inscribed on a stone pillar there:

If someone bearing the auspicious marks
will sprinkle this tank with blood from
his own neck, these statues of gold are his.

'"This message has been seen by everyone," said the spies,
"but none at all will accept such a heroic challenge. This
is the great marvel we saw."

'This king's curiosity was aroused immediately on
hearing this account, and he proceeded with the two spies
to the merchant's reservoir. The temple of the waterborne
god was located at its centre, and replicated well the
building skill of Viśvakarmā, the divine architect. On eight
sides of the temple were eight images of Bhairava, and
those of Lambodara and other deities were placed on the
border. The Lord of Dance, who is the beloved of the
goddess Chandikā was also installed there, his circling
arms flung out in a fierce tāṇḍava whirl.[1] In front of the
temple was to be seen a glistening stone pillar, fifty hands
in height including the pedestal, with a beautiful image of
the god Vishnu as a boar on the top. The god Parameśvara
was located at a point on the bridge along with twenty-four
other images set up in the same place. Food offerings,
mainly cakes, were freely distributed at the temple, and
the seven golden statues with the inscribed verse had been
placed at its front.

'King Vikramaditya himself saw the enormous reservoir
and the enchanting tall temple of Vishnu the Waterborne.
Marvelling greatly, he said to himself: "If I sprinkle the
blood from my neck in this tank, it will get filled with
water. This will benefit all people. It is a time of glory for
me today, that I am in a position to help others. This body
is bound to perish. Who knows what will happen, and
when? Meanwhile I must fill this tank. Life is transitory,
but fame abides as long as the moon and the stars."

'Vikrama then went into the sanctum of the temple
before him, and offered worship and salutations to Vishnu

the Waterborne. "O god of the waters," he cried, "you desire blood from the neck of a man with the thirty-two auspicious marks. Be now satisfied with this blood from my neck, and fill this tank with water." And as he then put the sword to his throat, the god held the blade, and said: "I am pleased with you, O hero. Choose a boon."

'"If you are satisfied," the king responded, "then make this tank full of water for the benefit of all. But this, and my coming here, should not be known by anyone." "What depth of character and magnanimity does this man have!" said the god on hearing Vikrama's reply. And the king returned to his capital. In the morning the people rejoiced to see the tank full, and the golden statues still standing there. "O how has this water come here!" they kept saying.'

After telling this tale, the statuette said to King Bhoja: 'Your Majesty, sit on this throne if you are also possessed of such magnanimity, benevolence, heroism, worth and similar virtues.'

9. A Courtesan Rescued

*O*nce again the time was propitious with a favourable planetary aspect, and the king came up slowly to the throne. Observing his intention, another statuette intercepted him, saying 'Listen!' and recounted the ninth tale.

'When Vikrama was the king, his minister was Bhatti, Govinda was the deputy minister, Chandra the commander-in-chief, and Trivikrama the court chaplain. This last had a son named Kamalākara who had always been spoilt. He enjoyed all the material comforts by his father's favour, eating rice with clarified butter and indulging himself with fine garments, jewellery, betel leaves and other luxuries, but he was devoid of learning. Once the chaplain told his pleasure-loving son, his own heart melting with despair, "O Kamalākara, how can you live in this wilful way, even after having been born a brahmin? The soul goes through hundreds of births in all kinds of species before obtaining a human form as the result of some good deeds. Even then, it is only by the greatest of merits that it is possible to be born in a brahmin family. Having attained this, you still follow evil ways. You are always out, and return home only at meal times. You behaviour is really quite improper. Moreover, this is the time for you to study and acquire knowledge. If you do not do this now, it will bring you to grief later. It is said,

Those who do not study and learn in childhood,
and spoil their minds with carnal pleasures in youth,
are despised in their old age as they wither away
like the lotus in the winter.

'"And similarly,

Those who have no learning,
nor penance, charity, merit,

virtue or even character:
they are just a burden on this earth,
mere animals wandering in the world
of mortals in the garb of man.[1]

'"In this world there is no greater adornment for man
than learning. As it is said,

Knowledge is in fact man's greatest beauty;
it is wealth, secret and secure; it provides
enjoyment, fame and happiness; it is a friend
in foreign lands, a guru of gurus,
a veritable god. Knowledge, not wealth,
is honoured by kings; without it
man is but a beast.

'"And similarly,

What does it matter if a person is from
a great family, if he has no learning?
It is the learned man who is honoured
in all the three worlds, even though
he has no family at all.

'"My son, you should acquire knowledge while I am still
alive. Learning will help you like your own family, once
you have it. It is said,

Learning protects one like a mother;
secures benefits for one like a father;
delights one and dispels sorrows like a wife.
It spreads fame and augments wealth.
It does indeed everything
which one's family should do."

'Kamalākara was filled with remorse on hearing his parent's

words. "I will not look my father in the face until I have learnt everything," the boy declared, and he went away to the land of Kashmir, the ornament of this earth.

'In Kashmir, Kamalākara went to the teacher Chandra Mauli Bhatta and saluted him with a prostration. "Master," he said, "I am but a fool. Having heard of Your Honour I have come here to study and to acquire knowledge. Have pity and instruct me, noble sir, so that I may become learned." Then he performed another prostration and, having been accepted by the teacher, commenced attending on him day and night. As it is said,

> Knowledge can be acquired
> by attending on the teacher,
> or by expending much money,
> or by building on other knowledge.
> There is no fourth way.

'Kamalākara spent a long time studying. Eventually the teacher condescended to teach him the incantation for propitiating the goddess of knowledge, which made him learned in everything. Taking the teacher's permission, he then commenced his journey back.

'On the way, Kamalākara came to the city of Kānchī, which was ruled by king Anangasena. In this city was a courtesan of incomparable beauty named Naramohini. Whoever saw her would be stricken mad with the fever of love, but whoever sought to sleep with her and enjoy her would die, as an ogre from the Vindhya mountain would drink up his blood.

'Having learnt all about these happenings, Kamalākara returned to the city of Ujjayini and went home to the embrace of his father, who trembled with emotion to see his son back, now versed in all the sciences, and piously saluting him. The parents and others held a great celebration, and on the following day Kamalākara went

with his father to the royal palace and saw King
Vikramaditya.

'The king was pleased with the mature talk of the
young man who had travelled abroad, and enquired about
his experiences. "I had gone abroad at my father's
direction," Kamalākara said. "There I studied in particular
the various sciences, the four Vedas with their ancillaries,
the secret learning illuminated in the three books,[2] and all
the arts which constitute good learning. When I was coming
back with my guru's permission, on the way I said to
myself: 'Even though I have obtained all this impeccable
knowledge, it is of no use as I have no fame. What should
I do?' Then, Great Emperor, in order to see the rulers
under Your Majesty's sway I went from king to king,
displaying my knowledge and receiving praise and honours
from them. Eventually I came to the city Kānchī, which is
ruled by king Anangasena. He treated me with respect and
I stayed for a month in the city. There I saw this marvellous
spectacle—"And then the young scholar truthfully narrated
to the king what he had gathered.

'"Come, Kamalākara," said Vikrama, "we both will go
there." And the king went with him to Kānchī, where he
saw Naramohini and was wonderstruck by her beauty.
Collecting himself somehow, he then told the clever
brahmin who stood close by: "Friend, what a great marvel!
I have never seen such good looks anywhere. This is
beauty personified. It gives man pleasure in one moment,
and pain in the next, like the vine which shimmers with a
golden glow but has poison inside. Now you and I should
investigate her inner inclinations. Go ahead, therefore,
and inform her that I will come to visit her."

'The brahmin carried out the king's instruction and
soon returned. "On my enquiry," he reported, "that
charming girl said: 'This is all right, but I have a problem.
I am in effect under the control of an ogre. So do what
you think proper under these circumstances.'"

'On hearing this reply, the king went boldly with the young man to Naramohini's pleasure-house. She washed his feet and welcomed him with unguents, perfumes and flowers. "O King, I am blessed today," she said, "my house is honoured. The dust from Your Majesty's feet has graced my courtyard.

> After a long time my house
> is favoured and honoured today
> with the touch of your noble feet.

'"Master, you must eat in my house," Naramohini added. "I have just eaten," replied the king. Then she offered him a betel leaf and they spent the night in conversation appropriate for the time. When only two watches remained Naramohini retired to rest, but the king remained within the house with the brahmin, and kept awake, fearlessly awaiting the ogre's arrival.

'The ogre came to Naramohini's house at midnight. A fierce maneater of terrifying aspect, he looked about and, having observed that the nubile beauty was stretched out at ease on her bed, sleeping quite alone, he went out of the house with a roar. The terrible sound shook up Naramohini, who followed him at once, wide-eyed with fear. Then the king called out loudly to the departing ogre. "I am here," he shouted, and the ogre turned back. The king grappled with him bare-handed. For a little while it was an equal fight, with blows and counter-blows. But King Vikramaditya had great strength. He felled the ogre to the ground and cut off his head with a saw for a weapon. Kamalākara rejoiced as he beheld the blessed king rise, piercing as it were the darkness which was the ogre. For the ogre was dark indeed, and only his fangs lit up the sky. He had now been put to sleep for ever by the king, and the young woman had been rescued.

'The tumult had meanwhile awakened Naramohini fully. Relieved to see the ogre lying dead, she praised the king, saying: "I was notorious as Naramohini, the enchantress of men in name, but actually their murderess by what I did. This reputation has now been demolished by Your Majesty. From today, master, I am at your disposal. Put me to whatever use Your Majesty wishes."

'The king was pleased to hear the courtesan. "If you agree," he told her, "then do what I say. You have all the signs of a lotus woman,[3] the best among the different categories of womankind. This Kamalākara is your equal. Therefore, good lady, accept him as your husband." With these words he gave away the beauty to the brahmin, and himself went back to Ujjayini, bright as the risen sun.'

After narrating this story, the statuette told King Bhoja: 'O King, sit upon this throne if you have such magnanimity, steadfastness, and capacity to help others.' And the king was speechless.

10. *The Gifting of the Magic Fruit*

*K*ing Bhoja radiated majesty like Indra, the lord of heaven. When he wished again to ascend the throne gifted by that god, yet another statuette spoke up: 'O King! Mount upon this lion throne only if you possess that kind of magnanimity. Otherwise do not be curious.

'In olden days, when King Vikramaditya ruled the earth, a wandering monk once came to Ujjayini from another land. He was versed in all kinds of learning, including the Vedas, the śāstras, medicine, astronomy, mathematics and dramaturgy. In short, he knew virtually everything and there was none to compare with him.'

'The king heard of the monk's reputation by word of mouth, and sent his chaplain to summon him. The priest went to the monk and saluted him. "Master," he said, "the king has asked for Your Holiness. You should visit him." The monk replied: "Learned sir, what do we have to do with seeing the king?

We live on alms,
sleep on the ground,
and need no clothes.
What will we do with princes?

'"Moreover,

Those who want nothing cannot be courtiers,
nor those without desires love honours;
the guileless will not flatter, and
the straightforward will not deceive."

'The chaplain repeated before the king what the monk had stated. On hearing it the king said to himself:

"Those who are free of desires
and intent only on the ultimate reality;
who have renounced all attachments
and shed all pride; whose one wish
is to stay content: such people
please themselves, not the world.

But those who long inwardly for
material enjoyments, who are covetous
at heart though outwardly detached:
such disguised and hypocritical rogues
charm the minds of the people."

'The king then went himself to see the monk. Saluting him, he took a seat and, in the course of their conversation, the monk explained every doubtful point on which the king questioned him. They discussed the science of the self and the subconscious memory of experiences in previous births; the method of regulating the breath by its systematic inhalation, retention and exhalation; and the sixfold practice of yoga with its eight branches of abstentions, observances, postures and breath control, withdrawal and concentration, meditation and trance. In continual talks with that great soul, the king learnt successively the Hatha Yoga, the Mantra Yoga, the Rāja Yoga, the science of controlling the body, and the Laya Yoga.

'Deeply satisfied, the king would go every day to discuss a variety of spiritual matters with the monk. "Master, how old are you?" he once enquired. "Why do you ask this, O King?" retorted the monk. "A man who knows the rules of conduct never reveals his age. Nine things should be kept private:

These nine one must keep secret:
age, wealth, domestic weakness,
charms, medicines, sexual relations,
gift, honours and disgrace.

'"Moreover, a master of yoga can bypass time and live long. I can teach you an incantation if Your Majesty has the strength to perform it."

'"What will I gain by learning your incantation?" the king asked. "By performing it you will be freed from old age and death," replied the monk. "Then teach it to me," the king said, "I will perform it."

'The monk taught the incantation to the king, and said: "Majesty, recite this for one year, during which you must remain celibate and perform the tenfold fire sacrifice with dūrvā grass shoots. At the time of the final oblation, a person will emerge from the fire pit bearing a fruit, and give it to you. Eat it, and you will have an impeccable body free from old age and death." Then he went away.

'Having learnt the incantation, and given the monk the fee due to a guru, the king proceeded to a forest as directed by him. There he stayed, subsisting on wild fruit, clothing himself in tree-barks, and letting his hair grow. Every day he would perform the three ritual ablutions, devotedly recite the incantation, and feed the sacrificial fire with dūrvā shoots as well as honey and sesamum seeds. One year passed thus. Then a dark blood-hued being emerged from the fire pit, gave the fruit of immortality to the king, and disappeared.

'This king took the fruit and returned to the city. As he went on the highway, a brahmin offered him a benediction. The man's limbs were withered with leprosy. "O King," he cried, "for brahmins the king is truly charged to be in the place of mother and father. It is said,

The king is the friend of the friendless,
and the eyes of the blind.
He is both father and mother,
and the best reliever of distress.

'"You give relief to all who suffer. My body is being

destroyed by this disease. With its dissolution my religious rituals will also cease. For the body is the sole instrument for the performance of sacred rites." Saying this the brahmin, whose hands and feet had been wasted by the sickness over time, emitted a sigh and begged the king for some medicine to save his life.

'The king said to himself: "I do not have any medicine here, and this man will not be able to get to the city. What should be done? In ancient times kings would give even their own dear lives to supplicants and gain lasting glory. This sick brahmin is not asking me for wealth, for my person, or for my life which is so hard to part with: he is asking only for medicine. It will be fitting for me to save him by giving him this fruit. This indeed is the best course for me." Thinking thus, the king gifted the fruit to the brahmin while explaining its powers, and himself went on his way to Ujjayini. He was indeed the foremost of the great philanthropists. A king who cannot compare with him is unworthy of this throne.'

11. An Ogre Reformed

*W*hen the king came forward once again to mount the throne, a statuette spoke out as before to restrain him: 'Pay attention! I will tell you a story.

'King Vikramaditya was a sovereign of impeccable valour and nobility. He had conquered all his foes. Once he placed the burden of government on his ministers and himself set out to travel abroad in the guise of a yogi. For,

> To see various kinds of marvels,
> to gain knowledge of the differences
> between good and wicked people,
> and to understand one self:
> these are the reasons for travel.

'The king would stop for some days wherever it pleased him, and also spend time where there were marvels to see. As he travelled thus, one evening the sun set while he was in a great forest, and he sat down for shelter under a tree.

'At the top of the tree lived an aged king of the birds named Chiranjīvī. His sons and grandsons would go out every day in the morning to feed themselves, and return in the evening, each one bringing a fruit for the old patriarch. It is well said,

> An old father or mother,
> a faithful wife, and an infant son
> must be looked after, says Manu,
> even if they do a hundred things wrong.

'From under the tree, the king listened to Chiranjīvī as, sitting at ease, the latter asked the other birds: "Children, what strange things did you see while wandering in various lands?" One bird replied: "I did not see anything extraordinary, but there is a great sorrow in my heart today." "Then tell us why you are sad," said Chiranjīvī. "How will just telling help?" asked the bird, to which the ancient replied: "My son, one who is sad can find relief by talking about his sorrow to a friend. It is said,

> One can find relief by telling one's sorrow
> to a steadfast friend, a virtuous servant,
> a sympathetic wife, and a congenial master."

'On hearing these words, the younger bird explained his grief: "Listen, father. There is a mountain called Śaivāla Ghosha in the northern country. Near it is the town of Palāśa. An ogre living on that mountain would come every day to the town, seize any man he chanced upon and take him back to devour him. Eventually the people of the town told the ogre: "O Bakāsura, do not be willful and eat just anyone who comes your way. We will give you one person everyday for your food." Much time has passed since then, and they surrender to him daily one man from each household in turn. Today a friend of mine is marked to be the ogre's diet, and this is the reason for the sorrow in my heart. I grieve because I can do nothing to prevent it."

'To the question "How did you become friends with a human?" the bird answered at length. "Being unable to help, how can I say this without feeling ashamed? Still, since you insist, I will tell you, unlucky though I am. Once a wicked birdcatcher had stretched out a sturdy net across a gully. It was my luck to be caught in it like a fool while I moved about above the water with my companions in search for food. Shortly afterwards a young brahmin came there to gather firewood and saw me. He felt sorry for me, and stood still for a moment, collecting himself. Then the good man came to me quickly and, full of compassion, cut the net and saved me and my companions. Thanks to him I am now alive. There were about twenty meshes in the net, and on my own I had not cut through more than five.

Such a benefactor is like a breath of life for me, and I am a wretch who can only feel sorry that he is to be devoured by the ogre today."

'After listening to the birds, the king went to the town of Palāśa. There, in the evening, he saw the man who had come according to his turn. He had given his final instructions to his family, and was sitting on the rock in front of the ogre's abode, his face miserable with the fear of death. "You there!" cried the noble Vikrama, "go away! I am here in your place today." "Who are you?" the man replied, "why do you want to die?" "What is it to you, who I am?" the king said with compassion. "Just go!" And the man departed, acknowledging the king's goodness.'

'The king then inspected the killing rock and, having bathed in a nearby lake, came and sat down on the stone. The ogre arrived at the same time. Astonished to see Vikrama sitting there benignly, he said: "From where have you come, great hero? Those who sit daily on this rock are dead with fright even before I arrive. But you seem to have tremendous fortitude. You are smiling. What is more, a man's faculties droop and decline when he is about to die, but you are radiant and beaming. So tell me who you are, sir?"'

'"Ogre," said the king, "what do you have to do with such considerations? Do your own business. Take your food. For,

> People tremble before death, mostly
> because they have not done their duties.
> Those who have done what they should
> await the arrival of death
> like that of a friend."

'"This is a good man," the ogre said to himself, "he grieves in the grief of others, setting aside his own wishes for pleasure and enjoyment. It is said:

The good wish for the happiness of all.
They grieve deeply in the grief
of others, abandoning their own
desires for pleasure and enjoyment.

'"Great one," he said to the king, "in giving it up for others, your life itself is worthy of praise. For,

Animals too live just to fill their bellies.
That life alone is praiseworthy,
which is lived for others.

'"Great hero," the ogre continued, addressing the king. "I am pleased with you. Choose a boon." The king then replied: "If you are happy with me, ogre, then give up eating humans from today. Furthermore, listen to my advice. Thus,

Just as life is dear to oneself,
so it is to all creatures.
Therefore the wise should protect
all living beings from the fear of death.

Similarly,

In this dread ocean of the worldly round,
people are forever tormented by the
sorrow of birth, old age and death;
for they are afraid of dying.

'"Moreover,

Just as you love your own life,
so do others love theirs.
Just as you guard your own life,
do the same for the lives of others."

'Instructed by the king, the ogre gave up killing creatures from that time. And, unnoticed by anyone, King Vikramaditya returned to his own Ujjayini.'

After recounting this story, the statuette told King Bhoja: 'Majesty, if you have such qualities of magnanimity and doing good to others, then sit upon this throne,' But the king stayed silent.

12. The Curse on the Callous Wife

*O*nce again when Bhoja approached the throne to mount it, a statuette restrained him, saying gently: 'O King, give me your attention for a moment and listen to my words.

'When Vikramaditya was king, in his capital city there lived a merchant named Bhadra Sena whose wealth was beyond measure. This man, who was no spendthrift, had a son called Purandara.'

'In course of time Bhadra Sena died. Purandara inherited all his father's property and, in keeping with his years, began to fritter it away. Once his dear friend Dhanada told him: "O Purandara, even though you are a merchant's son, you spend money like a scion of the high nobility. This does not become someone born in a trader family. A merchant's son should accumulate wealth, even if he is single; he should not waste even a cowrie.[1] The wealth a man accumulates will be useful in times of calamity. It is said:

It is only the man of wealth
whose desires get fulfilled.
Poverty has nothing.
A poor man is as good as dead
even though he may be alive.

Do not spend money for nothing.
On this earth the rich are happy,
even though they may lack
learning, penance and other virtues.

For those immersed in the ocean of problems,
wealth is the means of rescue.
So give up these childish ways, boy.
They lead to no good."

'After hearing this advice, Purandara said: "Dhanada, anyone who says that accumulated money is useful in a calamity is out of his mind. When calamities come, the wealth which has been acquired is also destroyed. The man of discrimination should neither grieve for what is gone nor worry about what is to come, but think only of the present. Similarly, it is said,

> One should neither grieve for the past,
> nor worry about the future.
> The wise work for the present.

'"For what will happen will happen even without any effort, and what had to pass will have similarly passed away. It is said,

> What has to be will certainly be,
> like the milk inside the coconut fruit;
> and what had to go has gone,
> like the wood-apple eaten by
> the elephant, as they say.

> The greedy man piles up money
> like a broom which sweeps together
> the grain scattered on the ground;
> better than him are those who
> donate or consume what they have.

> The wise have said that if one's money
> is neither enjoyed nor given away,
> it then becomes the root of calamities."

'Dhanada had no answer to these words, and he kept silent. Purandara then expended all his father's money and became a pauper. His relatives and friends respected him no longer; they would not even speak to him. "Oh, these friends and others attended to me as long as there was money in my hands," he thought to himself, "Now they do not speak to me. This is the true guideline: only one who has wealth has friends and their like. It is said,

> One who has wealth has friends
> and relatives, is considered learned
> and indeed a man by the people.

'"And, similarly,

> Kinsmen do not behave as before
> with a man whose wealth is gone.
> His attendants, who were there
> only because of his position,
> go their own way. His friends
> become fickle. What more can be said?
> For certain, even the wife
> does not have the same respect
> for one whose wealth is gone.

'"Similarly,

> The man who has money is well born.
> He is wise, learned, a connoisseur.
> He alone is eloquent,
> and he is good looking.
> All virtues depend on gold."

'Thinking thus, and unable to look his kinsmen in the eye, Purandara quit Ujjayini and went wandering to Madhurā. Not far from that city was a forest of bamboos. At night Purandara slept on a bench at a house in an outlying village.

'At midnight there came screams of a woman from the bamboo forest: "Save me! People, save me! This ogre is killing me!" In the morning Purandara asked the villagers: "What is there in this bamboo forest? Who was that woman weeping there?" They said: "Sounds of such weeping are heard every night in the forest here. But, out of fear, no one goes there to find out what it is."

'After his wanderings Purandara returned home and met the king who asked about his welfare. Eager to tell his curious story, he recounted it to the best of his knowledge. "Sire," he said, "my father had lived at Your Majesty's glorious feet. I gave away all the wealth that he had accumulated to supplicants, and was living in hardship without money. Crushed by the devil of poverty, and wanting to visit places of pilgrimage, I renounced my home and left the city. I wandered at will upto the Himalayas and, coming out of Kedāra, arrived at Madhurā. With its wealth and prosperity it is as lovely as the city of the gods. I roamed about there and slept at night at some woman's house when I heard these screams far away." Purandara then related the goings-on in the bamboo forest. On hearing of this marvel, the king went with him to the city of Madhurā.

'At night the king also heard the sound of a woman weeping in the bamboo forest. He went into the wood, and saw a most terrible ogre about to kill a helpless woman who was in tears. "You villain!" he cried, "why are you killing this helpless woman?" "What have you got to do with this?" the ogre retorted. "Go your own way. Otherwise you will die by my hand for nothing."

'The king rebuked the ogre in heroic words. "Know that I am Vikramaditya," he said. "What man dare harm a woman while I protect the people? Free this lady. Otherwise, listen, I will split your breast with the edge of my sword today and wash away your demons, vampires and witches in a stream of blood. Such will be your fall today that it will rend the earth and recall the crash of thunderbolts at the end of time."

'The ogre's lips trembled with rage at the king's wrathful words, and his long fangs lit up the darkness. "Do not brag before me, you little wretch of a petty prince!" he roared. "If you have valour then show it! My name is Narātikabala, and I am descended from Dundubhi.² You do not know me, you fool. Can I be killed with blows of a club? Look between the fangs in my mouth! The bones of people like you are already stuck there, and have yet to be dislodged."

'Having proclaimed their prowess loudly to each other, the two champions, Vikramaditya and the ogre, then clashed together like great bellowing bulls or angry tigers. They fought each other like two rutting elephants, and an extraordinary battle ensued with marvellous manoeuvres and a fierce exchange of blows which produced showers of sparks. Their bodies were crimsoned with blood from the wounds they inflicted on each other, so that they looked like two hills of red chalk. The tremendous sound of their combat and the terrible blows of their clubs filled the sky, as if with applause. By his personal strength the mighty king eventually killed the ogre, beheading him swiftly with his scimitar, after piercing him with its point.

'The woman then came up to the king and fell at his feet. "Master", she said, "my curse has ended by your grace. You have rescued me from a great ocean of misery." "Who are you?" the king asked. "Listen," she replied. "There used to be a brahmin of great wealth in this very city. I was his wife. But I was wanton. He loved me deeply, but I had no regard for him. Proud of my beauty, I would refuse whenever he asked me to sleep with him. Tormented by desire all his life, my husband cursed me at the time of his death. 'No, you wicked and villainous woman! Just as you have tortured me all my life, so will a hideous ogre from the bamboo forest do to you. Every night he will rape and murder you.' Thus was I cursed, and I beseeched him to limit it. 'No, my lord, grant me an end to this curse.' He then said: 'You will be freed from it when some man of great fortitude, who helps others, comes and kills the ogre.' So now I have been released by you. My life is ending, and I have nine jars full of gold which will go waste. It is a trifle for you, but please take them." She then told the king where the gold was kept and breathed her last.

'In a sporting gesture, the king presented the nine jars full of gold to Purandara the merchant, and went back with him to Ujjayini. King Bhoja, if you have such daring, heroism and great magnanimity, then grace this lion throne.'

13. The Gift of Merit

*O*n another occasion, when King Bhoja was again about
to ascend the throne after making all the arrangements
for his coronation, the thirteenth statuette said: 'O King,
one who sits upon this throne must have magnanimity like
Vikramaditya.'

Asked by the king what that magnanimity was like, the
statuette said: 'Listen, Your Majesty, once Vikramaditya
placed the burden of government on his ministers and
himself set out to travel around the world in the guise of
a yogi. He would stop for one night in a village and for
five in a town. Travelling thus, he came to a town near a
river which had a temple on its banks. All the people
there were listening to a preacher read from the purāṇa
scriptures. The king bathed in the river and went to the
temple where, after saluting the deity, he too sat down
near the congregation. At that moment the preacher
recited the following from the purāṇa:[1]

"This body is not permanent.
Nor is prosperity perpetual.
Death is always round the corner.
Therefore one must accumulate
a store of dharma.

Listen, this is the totality of dharma
as enunciated in the scriptures:
virtue is doing good to others;
sin is causing others pain.

That man is just a beast who,
even after having obtained birth
as a human being on this earth,
does not engage in doing good to others.

That man is truly a man whose wealth
is given to the needy, whose strength
is used to protect the imperilled,
and whose life is spent
in reviving the people.

A man with kindness in his countenance,
tenderness in his gaze,
and gentleness in his speech
stands first amongst good people

Speak truthfully and kindly,
without arrogance and abuse,
baseness and guile,
harshness and vilification.

There are many ways for men
to attain dharma in this world;
but the greatest is the protection
of those who come for refuge."

'While this recitation was taking place, a certain brahmin and his wife were crossing the river and got swept away in its torrent. Shouting and screaming, the brahmin cried out to the people listening to the purāṇa: "Oh! Oh! Good people! Run! Run! I am an old brahmin. My wife and I are being swept away forcibly by the river's current. Is there any pious hero who will save our lives?"

'All the people heard the cries of the couple being carried away in the water. They watched curiously, but none tried to save the two, nor enter the river to pull them out from the flow. King Vikramaditya, however, assured them, calling out: "Do not be afraid!" He jumped into the river, pulled out the brahmin and his wife from its great flood, and brought them to the shore while the people looked on and shouted in amazement.

'When the brahmin had regained consciousness he spoke to the king: "Great hero, my body here had been engendered by my parents in the past. Now you have given it a second birth. If I do not reciprocate your great kindness in saving our lives, my life itself will have been futile. I spent twelve years telling the rosary of the three holy names[2] in the waters of the river Godavari. The merit I accumulated thereby, I give to you. Furthermore, please accept whatever merit I have acquired by the difficult lunar fast and other rites."

'After the brahmin had spoken thus, his limbs trembling with emotion, the king replied with a respectful bow: "I am born in a kshatriya[3] family, and cannot accept reciprocal favours. I did not help you with the expectation of any return. For kshatriyas who follow the righteous path ordained for them, protecting people is their bounden duty. It is for that reason, learned sir, that I acted as I did. Do not think that I considered you will reciprocate my action."

'Hearing these calm and lofty words transfused with magnanimity, the brahmin realized that this was Vikramaditya. "Sire", he replied, "now I know that you are Vikramaditya. What other kshatriya would have such a heart? What Your Majesty has said is both proper and true. Nevertheless pay attention to my words. In the beginning Brahmā had created people from his head, arms, thighs, and feet, and ordained that they should all help each other. But only the brahmins and the kshatriyas were in particular called to help and protect one another as has been prescribed. Therefore it will be quite proper for you to accept my request on which I insist." On his insistent words the king agreed, and the brahmin blessed him and handed over all his accumulated merit before going away with his wife.

'An extremely hideous brahmin demon[4] then came up to the king. "Who are you, great one?" the king asked on seeing him. "I was a brahmin in this very town," the demon replied. "But I lived always by accepting tainted gifts and conducting forbidden sacrifices. I was also arrogant about my learning, and used to slander all the old and senior hermits. Because of these sins I became a brahmin demon and live on this fig tree out in front. I have been living there in great misery for the last ten thousand years. Today, having overheard the conversation between you two, I have come to you, sir, for Your Majesty is like a great tree, a benefactor of the whole world."

'"What do you want?" the king asked. The brahmin demon replied: "Please give me the merit which that brahmin has just given to you. With it I will be able to cross this terrible ocean of my past misdeeds." And the king gave him the store of merit that very moment. With it the brahmin demon was freed from his karmas and, assuming a divine form, he went to heaven, singing the king's praises. The king thereafter returned home.'

Having narrated this story, the statuette said: 'O King, if you have such magnanimity and ability to do good, then sit upon this throne.' But the king hung his head on hearing these words.

14. Fate or Endeavour

' *L*isten well, Your Majesty,' a statuette addressed King
Bhoja as before when he came forward once again to
mount the auspicious seat. 'Once upon a time King
Vikramaditya left his capital city to travel around the
world, reflecting in his mind that one who wishes to purify
himself should visit all the places of pilgrimage, temples
and penance groves that there are.'

'Travelling thus, the king came to a certain city and
stopped outside for a short while. There he saw a charming
park, with a temple dedicated to the goddess Pārvatī and
a river golden with water lilies. Having bathed in the river
and paid homage to the goddess, as he was coming out a
yogi named Avadhūta Vāsa arrived there. The king greeted
him and sat with him in the temple.'

'"May you be happy," said the yogi, "from where are
you coming, sir?" "I am just a pilgrim on my way," replied
the king. "Indeed!" said the yogi, "You are King
Vikramaditya. I saw you once in Ujjayini, so I know. Why
have you come here?"

'"O yogi," the king replied, "I had this idea in my
mind, that by travelling around the world one may see
some marvels, and also meet some great and good people."
But the yogi said: "O King, how could you be so careless
as to thus leave your kingdom and go travelling abroad?
What will you do if something untoward happens
meanwhile?"

'The king said: "I have come after placing all the
burdens of government in the hands of my ministers."
"Even so," the yogi retorted, "this violates the rules of
policy. It is said,

> The rulers who hand over the burdens
> of government to their officials and go
> wandering where they please are as foolish

as the people who go to sleep after putting
pots of milk before a horde of cats.

'"Furthermore, one should not neglect the kingdom
thinking that all is under one's control. Even if it is, one
should strengthen one's hold. Thus it is said,

One should hold fast to farming and learning,
the merchant and the wife,
one's wealth and one's kingdom,
as to the head of a venomous serpent.

'"This is what the rules of policy say," the yogi concluded,
"so be careful. Otherwise the kingdom may be lost, and so
may the king himself. Your Majesty should return to
Ujjayini, and not wander here."

'Though urged by the yogi, the king had an
independent mind. "My lord," he responded, "what Your
Holiness says is doubtless in accordance with proper policy.
But the mental makeup of men varies. Ends are attained
in two ways: fate and human endeavour. Belief differs
about which of the two is more important on this earth.
Men hoping for results are of three kinds: those who
believe in fate, those who depend on effort and those
inclined towards a combination of both. The proud ones
believe in effort alone, the wise ones in the power of fate,
and those in the middle try to gain their ends by both
means. Humans generally give up their effort at some
point, but fate is unstoppable. Whatever we have to get we
obtain by destiny's power, like the Dravida king who got a
kingdom effortlessly by the grace of the five forest spirits.
This demonstrates what I say."

'On being asked by the yogi, the king then told him
the story from the beginning.'

The Draviḍa King

There was a king of the Draviḍa country named Rāja Śekhara who was driven out of his kingdom by his enemies. He was going on foot with his senior queen to some other land when night fell and he stopped on the way under a tree near a city. At that time there were five forest spirits conversing with each other on the tree. 'The master of this city will die tomorrow morning,' they said, 'who will get this kingdom then?' One of them observed: 'It is given to the person who is asleep below this tree.'

The king and his spouse were pleased to hear this glad tiding. In the morning the king went to the city mentioned by the spirits. He washed himself in the waters of a stream in a park on the outskirts, performed the sacred rites and paid homage to the rising sun. Then he sat down, wide-eyed, on a handsome stone seat near a statue of the monkey god Hanumān at the crossroads.

Meanwhile the king of that place died childless, and the ministers let loose a female elephant carrying a garland to find another ruler. The animal saw Rāja Śekhara, placed the garland round his neck and, seating him on its back, carried him to the palace. All the ministers then assembled and anointed Raja Sekhara, establishing him as the monarch of the realm, where he reigned untroubled.

Once all the rival kings joined hands and came to the city to extirpate Rāja Śekhara. At that time the king was playing at dice with his queen. 'My lord,' she said, 'why is Your Majesty keeping quiet?' The rival kings have invaded the city and it looks that in the morning they will seize us too. Do something!'

'You simpleton!' said the king, 'what will come of doing anything? All work gets done by itself when fate is favourable, and it also destructs by itself when fate is not. Haven't you experienced this? Nothing else but fate is the ultimate cause of both growth and decay. It is said,

The undefended will live if protected by fate.
The well-defended will perish
if stricken by destiny. The orphan
survives though abandoned in the forest;
at home, he may not, even with precautions.

'Do not be afraid, my dear, just roll the dice. For,

The five spirits on the tree
both give and take away.
Roll the dice, fair lady,
what is to be will be.'

These words were heard by the five mighty spirits who said
to themselves: 'Those who gave this kingdom must also
protect it in every way. There is no doubt that one who
does not protect what he gives, nor defend that which
comes to him for refuge, will fry in some terrible hell.'
They then created a great fear of conspiracy in the minds
of the enemies who all became suspicious of each other
and were destroyed, fighting among themselves. Thereafter
King Rāja Śekhara continued to rule unopposed.

'This was the story that Vikramaditya narrated. Very pleased
to hear it, the yogi blessed the king and presented him
affectionately with a lingam of moonstone from Kashmir,
which provided whatever wealth one desired. Vikramaditya
too was satisfied and started back for his own city after
taking leave of the yogi. On the way back he was observed
by a brahmin who cried: "I wish you prosperity and good
luck. I am a poor man in need of money. Give me some,
O best of beings, so that I may eat something." And to this
brahmin who was begging for food, the king gave the
moonstone lingam from Kashmir, also explaining its power.'

After recounting this tale, the statuette said to the king: 'Your Majesty, sit upon this throne if you have such magnanimity and other virtues.' But the king listened and remained silent.

15. A Friend Indeed

Ш hen the lord Bhoja once again wished to ascend the throne, a statuette restrained him with sweet words: 'Your Majesty may mount this lion seat only if you have such courage, fortitude and magnanimity as did Vikramaditya.'

'When Vikrama was king, his chaplain was Vasumitra.[1] He was exceedingly handsome, versed in all the arts, and very dear to the king. He was also a benefactor of others, much loved by all people, and extremely rich.

'Once Vasumitra proceeded abroad to visit various places of pilgrimage. He went to Vārānasī and paid homage to Viśveśvara, the lord of the world, and then to Prayāga where he had the ritual bath during the month of Māgha.[2] After performing the ceremony for the ancestors at Gayā, he turned homewards and halted at a city on the way.

'This city was ruled by a celestial nymph who was under a curse and had no husband. A wedding pavilion stood there at a great temple to the deities Lakshmi-Nārāyana. By the gate of the temple was an enormous iron cauldron of boiling oil. The men appointed there would tell the people coming from outside: "If some hero will throw himself into this boiling oil, the nymph Manmatha Sanjivini will place the nuptial garland round his neck and take him for her husband."

'Vasumitra was enchanted by the beauty of the nymph. Returning home, he met all his kinsmen who were glad to see that he had come back safely. In the morning he went to the royal palace and met the king, presenting him with water from the Ganga and sacred mementos of Viśveśvara, before taking a seat.'

'"Well, Vasumitra," the king asked, "did your pilgrimage go well?" "By your favour, master," he replied, "I have returned safely after performing the pilgrimage." "And what new things did you see in those other lands?" the

king asked further. Vasumitra then told him about the
celestial nymph and the pot of boiling oil.

'The king's mind was filled with curiosity. He went to
the city with Vasumitra, saw the situation there and realized
that his friend had fallen in love with the nymph. He then
leapt into the cauldron. His body turned into a lump of
flesh as the people there raised a mighty hue and cry.
Hearing it, the nymph Manmatha Sanjivini arrived with
nectar which she sprinkled on the fleshy mass, reviving the
king with even greater beauty and radiance than he had
before.'

'"O best of heroes," said the nymph, "this vast kingdom
is yours. All that I have belongs to you. I am your slave.
Use me as you will." The king was pleased with her words.
As the siren was about to put the garland round his neck,
he said: "O Manmatha Sanjivini, if you have become mine,
then listen to me." "Speak master," she replied, "and I will
obey you in every way." "If you will do what I say," the king
told her, "then marry this chaplain of mine."

'"Blessed are you, king of kings," said the nymph,

"All this triple world is subject
to that steadfast man, whose heart
cannot be pierced by the arrows
of beauty's sidelong glances, nor
burnt by the fire of anger, nor
pulled out by the noose of greed.

'"So be it," she said, and placed the nuptial garland round
the chaplain's neck. The king then had them married and
appointed Vasumitra as the ruler of that kingdom, before
returning to his own capital.

'O King, if any man had such courage, prowess and
magnanimity, he would be competent to mount this
throne.'

16. A Springtime Gift

*O*nce more, when the king came forward to mount the throne, a statuette intervened, saying: 'Illustrious men like Your Majesty should hear about this deed of King Vikramaditya which dispels all evil.

'Once King Vikramaditya set out to conquer all the quarters of the earth. He traversed the east, the south, the west, the north and all the intermediate directions, bringing the local kings under his sway. Taking the elephants, horses and other valuables they proffered in tribute, he reestablished them in their respective domains, and then turned back to his own capital.

'At the time of the king's entry into the city, the astrologers told him: "Sire, there is no auspicious moment for entering the capital for the next four days." On hearing this he halted outside and, having tents erected in a park, began to spend the four days there itself.

'Spring had meanwhile arrived. It is the king of the seasons, and with it:

The bakula trees suddenly burst
into blossom, as if, people say,
having had mouthfuls of wine sprayed[1]
on them by celestial nymphs with lovely eyes.
And bees swarm around them from all sides.

'And,

The bees gather with a gentle hum,
attracted by the mango blossom's
mild but heady nectar;
and a soft breeze wafts for ever,
redolent with the perfume of lovely women.

'Seeing this revelry of spring, the minister Sumantra came to the king and said: "Sire, spring, the king of the seasons, has arrived. The vernal rites should now be performed to propitiate all the seasons, dispel all misfortune, and ensure everyone's prosperity." "Then I will gladly perform them tomorrow," the king replied, "please make all the arrangements."

'The excellent minister arranged everything as ordered by the king. He had a pavilion decorated with cloth, ornamental arches and flowers. It shone with jewelled pillars and a rich canopy of bright fabrics, and at its centre he installed a great gem-studded throne. The following morning he told his august master: "Sire, everything is ready. Please proceed as you think proper."

'The pure-souled and meritorious king then went into the pavilion and prayed to the deities Umā and Maheśvara, Laksmi and Nārāyaṇa, as well as Madana, the god of love, and his consort Rati, and Vasanta, the divine embodiment of spring. He worshipped them with camphor, sandalwood, musk, orpiment, aloes wood and saffron; and with barley grains and the flowers of amaranth, jasmine, asoka and frangipani. He also honoured the brahmins in proportion to their intellect, and had the minstrels sing the Vasanta Rāga—the musical mode of spring.

'After listening to the music, the king proceeded with his retinue directly to the park. Enjoying himself with all manners of sports, at noon he went into a plantain grove which had been marked out with flags. There, seated upon a golden throne inside a pavilion bright with decorations, he gave attention to the subtleties of many arts, demonstrated in due order with great eagerness by thirty-six princes, each occupying his allotted place. He also had the pleasure of talking to learned scholars for a while.

'Thereafter, at the king's command, a preacher made a forthright speech to preclude any excess in preoccupation with the transient pleasures of this world. "O King," he said,

"What is the use of kingdom, wealth
and stores of grain; of personal ornamentation,
erudition, great strength and clever speech;
of a most excellent birth, a pure family
and an abundance of bright merits:
if the soul is not freed from the terrible
prison house of this worldly existence?"

'"Speak further, priest," said the king. And he continued:

"Difficult is the wordly path.
Ailments are hard to cure,
and death can come at any time.
It is difficult to decide
on proper action, and nothing to support
those who fall on the way. Anyone
who seeks the bliss of salvation
must reflect on this, day and night,
with a clear mind, and apply his thoughts
decisively to dharma."

'"Speak some more," said the king. The preacher continued:

"Even though they may endure for long,
sensual pleasures must inevitably fade away.
What difference does it make if people
will not give them up willingly?
If they cease on their own it grieves the heart
immeasurably; but if they are renounced,
it gives one the infinite happiness of peace."

'The king marvelled on hearing these words. "What this
priest says is true indeed," he thought, "for,

The very thoughts which could release
man from enjoying worldly pleasures,

bind him to them even more.
He knows that life is as transient
as a wave in the water, and is yet
attached to pleasure; that prosperity
can vanish like a dream, but still
wants to enjoy it for ever;
that youth is no more than a cloud, but still
continues to embrace women with passion."

'At this time an extremely aged man came into the royal assembly, leaning on a staff, and holding the hand of a girl who accompanied him. The king greeted this venerable brahmin and seated him on a chair. "From where have you come, brahmin," he asked kindly, "and on what business? Tell me." Thus addressed, the old man told the monarch: "O King, I have a petition." "Submit it then," said the king.

'The brahmin said: "I live in the town of Naṅdivardhana. Eight sons were born to me, but no daughter. With my wife I then made a vow before the goddess Jagadambikā, the mother of the world: 'O mother, if I have a girl child I will name her after you. Moreover, I will give her in marriage to a groom learned in the Vedas, together with her weight in gold.' Now here she is, and the time has arrived for her wedding. The planet Jupiter stands in the eleventh house, and this will not happen again in the coming year. I have come to you, knowing that there is no one else in the world apart from Vikrama who will give her weight in gold."

'"You did well, brahmin," said the king. "Take as much as you need for your work." He then called his treasurer and told him: "O Dravya Datta, give this brahmin his daughter's weight in gold. In addition, give him eight millions in gold for her eightfold ceremony."

'Dravya Datta gave the ordered amount of gold to the brahmin, who returned home with his daughter, entirely contented. The king too entered his capital at an auspicious time.

'O King, if you are also able to give as much to a supplicant who comes with a petition, then occupy this throne.'

17. Helping a Rival

*C*urious to hear another statuette speak, the king came forward, pretending to mount the throne. The statuette saw him and understood the purpose for which he had come. 'Listen, O King,' she said with a smile which lit up her face, 'to a tale of King Vikramaditya and his magnanimity, well known for the daring with which he did good to others.'

'No one had magnanimity and other virtues like Vikrama. Because of them his fame had spread over the three worlds. All supplicants praised only this king, for their blessings are indeed meant for donors rather than heroes. It is said,

> The blessing of those who seek wealth
> are indeed meant to please donors;
> it is the thunder of the battle drum
> which brings joy to heroes.

'Moreover, heroism, learning, religious work and other such virtues can occur everywhere, but not the virtue of renunciation. It is said,

> All animals can fight; the parrot,
> and the myna bird can talk;
> but the real hero and scholar
> is one who gives a gift.

'And further,

> Some have a heroic nature and some
> have compassion of heroic proportions;
> but they are not worth one-sixteenth
> of a person whose charity is heroic.

To give away `what is yours
is the one praiseworthy virtue.
With it, there is no need
for a mass of other virtues.
If animals, stones and trees
are honoured, it is because
of their renunciation.

The virtue of renunciation I consider
greater than a hundred other virtues.
If the person who has it is also adorned
with learning, what more can I say?
If he is heroic too, all homage to him.
And when all three are there without
arrogance, it is a marvel of marvels!

'All these four virtues obtained in Vikramaditya. Once a
bard recited a poem in his praise before another king. On
hearing it that king became jealous. It is said:

One without merit cannot understand
meritorious men; and one with merit
is jealous of them. Rare is the honest
person who both has merit
and is happy to see it in others.'

'"O bard," that monarch asked, "why is it that all bards
praise Vikramaditya alone? Is not there any other king?"
"Your Majesty," the bard replied, "there is no king like him
in the three worlds for giving and doing good to others,
for daring and heroism. He has no attachment even to his
own person in doing good to others."

'"I too will do good to others," the king said to himself
after listening to the bard. He then summoned with all
respect a certain saint and, after due courtesies, posed the
question in his heart. "Lord, how can I become greater

than Vikramaditya? We hear that he always gives more than he is asked for. Is there any method whereby new wealth can be created every day for doing good to others?"

'Having listened carefully to the wish expressed by this king, the saint said: "You should propitiate the circle of witches in the manner prescribed. After offering a hundred thousand oblations of melted butter into the sacred fire, you should offer your own person as the final oblation with this spell. Your object will then 'be achieved."

'The king then performed the worship of the witches' circle, and offered his own body as an oblation in the blazing fire to complete the rite. The witches were propitiated. They brought the king back to life and asked him to choose the boon he wished for. With clasped hands raised to his head in supplication, he requested that his seven mansions be filled every day with gold. "This will happen if you always perform this rite," said the witches, and granting him this boon, they vanished. Thereafter the king would everyday make an oblation of himself into the fire and receive a fresh body. With the wealth he thus obtained he would make gifts and do other charity as he pleased.

'When King Vikramaditya heard of this development from one of his spies, he went straight away to that ruler's capital and observed this situation. "This person should not have to undergo such suffering day after day," thought the compassionate king, who loved to do daring deeds. He went to the sacrificial house at a time when no one was there and, invoking the witches in his mind, commenced to offer his own body into the fire. In that very moment the circle of witches appeared before him and said: "O chief of heroes, there is no need for such daring. You have come here for the sake of someone else, and offer your own body to please us. This is not proper. Choose, we will give you whatever you want."

'Thus requested by the witches, the king, who was ever intent on helping others, chose the noblest of boons. "Let the seven mansions of this scion of kings be forever full of gold, without his suffering the agony of bodily sacrifice," he said. "So be it," replied the witches, and they granted the boon and disappeared. As for Vikramaditya, he returned to his capital without making public what had happened.

It is the small minded who calculate
"this is mine or another's".
For the large hearted the world itself is a family.

There is a certain great and extraordinary
sternness of heart in good people:
having done a good turn they flee
far away, afraid that someone
will return the favour they have done.

'Thus did people praise the king. That monarch alone may grace this throne who is able to act similarly.'

18. Vikrama Visits the Sun

*O*bserving that King Bhoja had again arrived desirous of mounting the throne, a statuette said: 'O King, only one with Vikrama's daring, fortitude and magnanimity is worthy of occupying this great throne of Indra.'

'Tell a tale of his magnanimity and other qualities,' asked the king. 'Listen, O King,' the statuette replied, 'Vikramaditya ruled without transgressing proper policy or departing from dharma.'

'Describe what is right policy,' the king said. 'Listen, O King,' said the statuette, 'in Maṇipura there was a brahmin named Govinda Śarmā. He knew the rules of proper policy, and would explain them every day to his son. I also heard him, and will tell you what he said.

'An intelligent man should never keep company with villains, for this can lead to great and repeated mishaps. It is said,

> The company of villains is the cause
> of repeated mishaps for good people.
> Here, what is known must be said:
> the lord of Lankā abducted the wife
> of Daśaratha's son, but the one who
> was arrested[1] was the southern ocean.

'What is prescribed, therefore, is the company of good people. There is nothing more beneficial in this world. It is said,

> Good people's company puts to shame
> the charms of sandalwood, moonlight
> and soft breezes. It dilutes depression
> and kindles joy. It also leads to prosperity.

'Another thing: have enmity with none. Others should not be oppressed. Servants should not be punished without fault. The wife should not be disowned except for some serious sin, for that is the way to everlasting hell. It is said,

> One who disowns an obedient,
> competent and soft spoken wife,
> who is the mother of a brave son,
> and in whom no sin has been found,
> will go to everlasting hell.

'One should not assume that prosperity is there to stay. Fortune is as unstable as water. It is said,

> Fortune is extremely fickle.
> If flickers like the candle's
> flame in a mighty wind.
> Therefore enjoy and give away
> your money, honouring
> the venerable and cultivating the good.

'Do not tell secrets to women. Do not worry about the future. Seek the benefit of even enemies. Do not let the day be wasted without charity and study. Serve your parents. Do not talk to thieves. Do not always give callous answers, nor take away a lot for the sake of a little. It is said.

> The wise man will not destroy the greater
> for the sake of the lesser. Wisdom
> lies in protecting the first with the second.

'Alms should be given to those in distress at holy places. Good should be done to others in thought and speech as well as action.

'This is how the rules of proper policy have been expounded for ordinary people,' said the statuette, 'but King Vikrama understood them all by his very nature.

'Once upon a time a certain foreigner came to see the king and took a seat. "O Deva Datta,"[2] asked the king, "where do you stay?" "O King," he' replied, "I am a foreigner. I stay nowhere in particular. I travel all the time." "And what are the new things you have seen in the course of your travels?" the king asked. "I saw a great marvel, O King," was the reply. "Tell me, what was it?" asked the king.

'"On the mountain where the sun rises," said the foreigner, "there is a great temple to Aditya, the sun god. The river Ganga flows there, with a holy ford for bathing, which destroys all sin and has satisfied many seekers. A pillar of gold emerges from the Ganga's current, with a throne studded with the nine gems[3] at its top. This golden column appears above ground level at sunrise, and grows to reach the sun's orb at noon. Then, as the sun begins to set, it descends by itself and sinks into the Ganga's stream. This is the great marvel which I saw; and it happens every day."

'A lion among kings, Vikrama was endowed with unique daring. He became curious on hearing the foreigner's account, and set out to see the marvel. He came eventually to the town called Kanakaprabha, full of golden towers and gateways of burnished gold, and the river renowned for washing sin away, which was known there as Sūryaprabhā or Solar Radiance. With a mind full of devotion, he bathed and purified himself in the river's eddies, and then worshipped the god Aditya, the lord of beasts, with flowers. After that he spent the night in the god's temple, keeping a fast. At dawn he arose with a tranquil mind, performed the ritual ablutions at the holy ford, and prayed to the sun. At that very time the golden pillar suddenly emerged from the water before his eyes.

'With a quick leap, the king got on top of the pillar which rose up swiftly as the sun ascended to the centre of the sky. When the pillar neared the sun, the latter's rays, which were like sparks of fire, scorched the king's body so that it began to look like a lump of meat. In that shape he reached the solar orb, and paid homage:

"Obeisance to the sun, the sole
light of the world, and the cause
of its creation, preservation and destruction.
He is the three-aspected, the embodiment of the three
   qualities,[4]
and the essence of the trinity
of Brahmā, Vishnu and Śiva."

'After chanting many other hymns of praise, the king fainted because of the solar heat. Pleased with his daring, the sun god sprinkled him with nectar and restored him to consciousness. "I am blessed," cried Vikrama. "You are more than a great hero," the sun god said, "you have reached this orb which has been unattainable by anyone at all. I am therefore pleased with you. Choose a boon." "O god," replied the king, "what greater boon can there be than this? I have reached your abode which is unattainable even by great sages. By your grace I have everything that I need."

'Much contented with the king's words, the sun god gave him his own earrings, studded with the nine gems, saying: "I am satisfied with you. Take this pair of my earrings. From the radiance of their rubies comes the light of my dawn. They will yield a shower of bright gold every day."

'The god departed after giving the two earrings to the king. As he moved on towards sunset, the pillar also sank back into the water. And the king went down with it, wishing to discover its root. This lay in the nether world, where he beheld the goddess Prabhā, beloved of the sun god and the mother of the world. Bowing to her, he stood there with utmost courtesy, and the goddess graciously gave him a divine jewel which produced ornaments at wish. Bowing to her repeatedly, he then withdrew from her presence and went out.

'Near the goddess, the king noticed the very same pillar of gold. It stood at the centre of a gilded altar, lit with towering flambeaux at night. Understanding its properties, the king sat upon it at dawn, and when it rose out of the river at sunrise as before, he jumped off and got to the riverbank.

'The high-minded king then broke his fast with due ceremony in the pavilion of the twelve Adityas right there. As he was on his way back, he spoke to a poor, emaciated brahmin beggar who was accompanied by his wife. The king was compassionate to the poor, and his words brought joy to the beggar. "Here, brahmin," he said, "this pair of earrings made of gems come from the sun god. They shower a quantity of gold every day. And this brilliant jewel is a mark of the goddess Prabhā's grace. It produces ornaments at wish. Take one of these two for yourself and give the other to your wife." Then he cheerfully explained their powers to the brahmin and, giving him the jewelled earrings, returned to the city of Ujjayini.'

'King Bhoja, if you have such daring, generosity and fortitude, then Your Majesty may mount upon this throne.'

19. The Visit to the Nether World

*A*s usual, a statuette addressed King Bhoja when he came up again to ascend the throne: 'O King, you may hope to mount this if you have his extraordinary fortitude and generosity. His virtues were envied even by the most virtuous. Listen, lord king, to what they were like.

'The noble king Vikrama reigned in the land of Avanti. Under his rule men were righteous, women were chaste, and people lived their full spans of life. The trees were always fruitful, the lands were fertile, and the clouds sent rains whenever needed. There was fear of sin, faith in virtue, hospitality to guests, reverence to gurus and remembrance of God. People gave to the deserving and adhered to state policy in their dealings.

'Once the king sat enthroned. The nobles and the princes seated in the assembly were of various kinds. Some had bards recite their genealogies. Some proud ones themselves lauded their own prowess. Some were bearded young men, versed in wielding the twenty-six offensive weapons, who jested with each other. Some were disposed to promote their dependents. Some were preoccupied with the next world, and others with accumulating merit in this one. Such were the lords who served the king.

'At that moment the chief of the hunters arrived for an audience. Swarthy, so that he looked virtually like darkness in human shape, he made a prostration and stood trembling with folded hands before the king. Prompted by the ushers, he said: "Sire, in the forest on the western side of Mount Mandara, there is a great boar which is always scouring the countryside. Such a mighty wild animal has never been seen before. It has taken abode there and troubles people all the time."

'The king was a keen hunter. On hearing the woodman's words, he proceeded with the princes to the forest. There, in a grove of blooming flame of the forest

trees by a stream, roamed the boar, happily nibbling at
sweet smelling mustā grass roots. Its pitch-black body
darkened the space behind it, while its gleaming tusks lit
up the front. It was like a dark mountain, shutting out the
light and turning all trees into ebony.

'Disturbed by the loud shouts of the soldiers and the
furious baying of the dogs, the boar came out of the
grove. All the princes discharged their twenty-six weapons
at it, eager to demonstrate their skills. But the powerful
beast dodged them all, broke through the canine pack,
and headed towards a mountain cave, pursued by the
king. Sword in hand, Vikrama alone followed it on his
swift horse, almost touching it at every step.

'The boar was blackness itself. As it plunged into the
cave it struck hard at the king, who dismounted and
tethered his horse at the entrance before continuing to
pursue the elusive animal. Inside the cave, he went forward
feeling the way with his hands as it was too dark for his
eyes. At last he saw a marvellously shaped doorway, gleaming
with gems in a mesh of light like the newly risen sun. But
there was no sign of the boar.

'"From where has this doorway come?" wondered the
king. "And where has the boar gone?" In that moment
there was tremendous noise like the roar which echoes the
thundering clouds of the final deluge, and the doorway
burst asunder to make a wide opening.

'His sword on guard, the king went down a descending
path on stairs of sparkling crystal lit with lamps. Foremost
of the heroes and the strongest of the strong, he continued
for long on that lonely descent. Finally, he saw before him
a city which delighted his eyes.

'It was surrounded by a golden wall with gates of
glittering ruby. It bathed the sky with the glow of its crystal
mansions. It shone night and day like sunrise, with the
splendour of its lovely palaces and their gilded stone
columns. Here rubies blazed like lamps to dispel the

mysterious shadows cast by pillars of sapphire. Here perfumed and passionate youths delighted in breezes wafting fragrance from the mouths of serpent maidens.

'As he came to its gate and beheld the city's glory, a chamberlain appeared and conveyed a royal summons. "King Vikramaditya! The sovereign lord of the nether world, Bāli, the rival of the gods, wishes to see you," he said, and conducted Vikrama inside, pointing out the wealth of the city. He then informed his master that the king had arrived.

'Coming to the royal portal, the king saw Krishna as the gatekeeper there. He said to himself:

"When the lord of the world came
before him as a little supplicant,
and the earth's globe was the gift
in question, it was the god who was
astonished by Bāli's modest smile.

'"This indeed is the city of King Bāli, to whose house Śri Krishna himself came as a supplicant and, obligated by the gift he received,[1] minds the gate even today." Announced by the chamberlain, he then entered the palace and saluted King Bāli.

'"O prince of givers of the Kali age, Vikramaditya, " said King Bali, "I am delighted that you have come, but what is the reason for your visit?" "O king of the giants," replied Vikrama, "I have come only to see you. There is no other reason." "If my lord has come out of friendship for me," Bāli said, "oblige me then by asking for something." "I lack nothing," Vikrama responded, "by your grace I have a sufficiency of everything." "My lord!" exclaimed Bāli, "when did I say that Your Majesty lacks anything! I spoke out of friendship, for the signs of a friend are thus described. It is said,

These are the six signs of affection:
to give and to receive;
to tell and to ask secrets;
to entertain and to be entertained.

There can be no affection
for anyone without some service
rendered; even the gods grant wishes
only in return for the gift of prayers."

'Having said this, the lord of the giants gave to the king an essence and an elixir before bidding him farewell. To assist him on the way out, he sent the very same attendant who had earlier assumed the shape of the boar. Escorted by this person, the king came back swiftly to where his horse stood at the entrance of the cave. Dismissing the giant, he remounted his horse and proceeded towards Ujjayini.

'On of the the way the king saw two brahmins who were distraught with hunger. They begged him for some rice and suchlike to eat. "I have nothing here except this magic essence and this elixir with divine powers," said the king. "Take one. The essence can turn all metals into gold, and the elixir is able to prevent old age and death."

'One of the two brahmins was old. "I am stricken with age, O King," he said on hearing the monarch's words. "Give me the elixir." But his son, who was a young man, said: "What is the use of the elixir? Give us the essence which produces gold." Then there commenced an unholy quarrel between father and son: "This is the best! That is the best! This is for me! That is mine!" Observing their argument, the king took pity and said: "O you two! Do not fight. Take both these things." And he gladly gave them the essence as well as the elixir. The two went away, praising him, and he too returned to Ujjayini.

'My lord, whoever has such generosity, daring and fortitude would alone be worthy of occupying this throne.'

20. An Example of Effort

'*B*est of rulers, listen to this wonderful tale,' said the next fair statuette as the king came to mount the throne.

'In providing protection to the land, it was King Vikramaditya's rule to travel abroad for half the year, and to foster welfare at home in the other half. In this way he governed the realm and also went out of the city and the country to see other lands. He travelled the whole earth from the Himalayas to the sea, observing with great interest all the holy places of pilgrimage and temples, the towns and the hilltops, and the beautiful forest regions bordering the rivers.

'Once when he had gone abroad, after visiting various lands the king came to a city called Padmālaya. Seeing a fine lake of very pure water in a park outside the town, he drank from it and sat down there. Other people, some of them strangers and some natives of the place, had also come there and were sitting similarly. "O we have seen many countries and places of pilgrimage," they were saying to each other, "we have climbed very difficult and inaccessible mountains. But in no place did we see a really great personage." "How can one be seen?" observed one of them. "It is impossible to go where a great saint may be. The roads are difficult. There are many hazards on the way. One may even lose one's life. And if one perishes in the beginning of an enterprise, who gets its fruit? For this reason the wise must protect themselves as the first priority. As it is said, the primary means of attaining dharma is one's own body. Thus,

Wives and wealth, land and sons,
good and evil actions can occur again
and again, but this body will not.

'"Therefore wise men will not take risks. Thus,

> The clever man does not commence
> works which are fruitless, difficult
> to finish, impossible, or where
> the expenses neutralize the profit.

For,

> Even in times of danger
> the wise man will not go
> up a difficult and terrible
> mountain full of serpents.

'"For, whatever is done should be done after due thought, and one should not undertake any work of which the end result will be minimal."

'The king was also listening to this conversation. "Why do you speak like this, O strangers?" he said. "Everything is difficult to obtain as long as a man does not act with manliness and courage. It is said,

> Courageous men do not just
> keep waiting for opportunities.
> Many desirable things may
> be hard to get, but can
> nevertheless be obtained,

'"Thus,

> Sometimes water falls into a ditch
> from the sky; but it can also
> come there from below.
> Fate is unimaginably powerful
> in this world, but is not
> manly effort powerful too?"

'"What should be done, then?" said those people, after listening to the king. "Tell us, great hero." The king replied: "If you go twelve leagues from this city, there is a cragged mountain in the middle of a great forest. At its top there lives a great master yogi named Trikāla Nātha. He gives whatever one desires if one can see him. I am going there." "We will come too," they said, and the king told them: "Come with pleasure."

'They then set out with the king. Finding the forest road extremely difficult to traverse, they asked him: "Great hero, how far is the mountain?" "Eight leagues more," the king replied. "Then we will go back," they said, "It is very far and the road is very difficult." "O strangers," said the king, "what is far for those on business? It is said,

> Nothing is too burdensome for the capable,
> and nothing too far for those
> on business. No land is foreign
> for the well educated, and none
> can be alien for those who speak sweetly."

'Having travelled for another six leagues, as they went ahead a frightful serpent with great gaping jaws spitting poisonous flames blocked their path. On seeing it the others took fright and ran away, but the king persisted in going forward. The serpent came up and bit him after capturing him in its coils. But, though encircled by the reptile, and swooning with the power of its venom, the king nevertheless climbed that most inaccessible of mountains and saw the yogi Trikāla Nātha, whom he saluted.

'At the mere sight of the yogi, the serpent left the king, who was also freed from its venom. "O great hero," said the yogi, "why have you come to this inhospitable place so recklessly and with so much trouble?" "O master," replied the king, "I have come only to behold Your worship." "Did you have much trouble?" the yogi asked. "None at all," said the king. "How could there be any trouble? At the mere sight of Your Worship all my sins have disappeared. I am blessed today, for it is very hard to get to see the great. What is more, one must work for self-improvement as long as the body and the senses are sound. It is thus said,

The wise should make every effort
to improve themselves as long as
this body is healthy and whole,
the faculties unimpaired,
old age still distant
and life not yet exhausted.
What is the use of attempting
to dig a well when the house
is already on fire?"

'The yogi was pleased to hear these words. He presented to the king a quilt, a crayon and a stick, explaining the powers of all three. With the crayon one could draw the picture of an army. It would come to life if touched with the stick held in the right hand, and carry out whatever was desired; when touched with the stick held in the left hand, it would vanish. The quilt would yield money, grain, clothing, ornaments and other things one wished for.

'The king accepted the gifts and took leave of the yogi after paying his respects. As he was coming back, he saw on the road a prince who was collecting wood for a fire he had built nearby. "Gentle sir," the king asked him," "What is this? What are you doing?" He replied:

"How can sorrow be explained
to someone who has not suffered it,
who cannot cure it, and who
does not feel it for another?"

'The king then said:

> "I have suffered sorrow,
> I am able to cure it,
> and I feel it for others.
> So, explain it to me."

'The prince then said: "You are a mirror which reflects the grief of others. I am the son of a king. My kingdom was taken away by force by my kinsmen. Unable to retaliate against them or to bear this humiliation, I am collecting firewood to immolate myself."'

'The king then gave him the crayon, the stick and the quilt and explained their magic qualities. Well contented, the prince saluted the king and went home. King Vikrama also returned to Ujjayini. It is said:

> Who can compare with
> Vikrama on this earth?
> He obtained from the yogi
> three things of great power
> which fulfill all desires,
> and gave them away
> to a king deprived of his kingdom.'

At these words of the statuette, the lord of the Bhojas stood for a moment frozen, like someone in a picture. Then he hung his head and again went back to the inner apartment.

21. The Eight Magic Powers

*W*hen the king again came forward to mount the throne, he was addressed by the next statuette: 'Your Majesty can neither ascend this throne of Indra, nor give it up. You only torment yourself. No man may occupy this great royal seat unless he has the generosity of Vikrama. If you wish to know what it was like, then pay attention to the deeds of that worker of wonders.

'During the rule of Vikrama there was a minister named Buddhisindhu, who had a son, Guhila by name. The young man lived like a prince, eating rice and melted butter, and did not study at all. He was a fool without a particle of sense. With the intention of disciplining him, his father once admonished him with some precepts:

"Empty is the home without a child,
the land devoid of kinsfolk,
and the mind of a fool.
And everything is empty for the poor.

Alas, my son, you were born
under some evil star. You are
a bad child who remains
unlettered. Because of you
I have become notorious
among those who have children.

How could I, so rich in learning,
have such worthless progeny?
It were better to have had
a barren wife or a stillborn child.

My boy, you obtained a human birth
because of past merits, but your mind

was stricken by fate. You have
neither learning nor discrimination."

'Guhila was mortified by his father's words. They pierced
his heart like arrows. Unobserved by anyone, he left home
that very night and went away to the province of Karnāta.
There, with hard practice, he mastered learning, which
brings both good sense and fame, and lived happily. After
some time he took leave respectfully from his teacher and
set out for home.'

'On the way he passed through the province of Andhra.
It was a land enriched by the Kākati kings with treasures
accumulated in their victorious campaigns. Here the
Godavari flowed through seven streams into the sea. This
river, also called Gautami, the purifier of the world, springs
from the matted hair of the god Śiva, and forms in this
place a holy ford know as Ushna Tīrtha or Hot Spring.
Rice cooks in no time when soaked in its water. There was
also a temple to the god, locally known as Ushneśvara,
which displayed the craftsmanship of some earthly
Viśvakaramā in all its diversity.

'The minister's son arrived there, thinking gloomily
how far he still was from his homeland. At midnight he
saw in the vicinity eight beautiful damsels, gleaming like
gold and the lightning. One was skilled in music and song,
and blew upon a wind pipe with the lotus bud of her mouth.
Another warbled sweet notes on a mellifluous flute, which
she held playfully to her lovely lips. Yet another played a
drum with her hands, keeping time with the melody. Some
sweet-voiced girls, adorned in diverse ways, sang a lilting
song based on the pure fifth note which completely
enthralls the mind. Others danced gracefully with an
enchanting display of the arousal of emotions, their limbs
swaying to the music and their feet keeping time.

'Guhila gazed at all this in wonderment. The damsels
too noticed him as they departed in the morning after

having worshipped the god Śiva Ushṇeśvara with music and dance. "Come, gentle sir," one of them called out, "we will go to our city." He obeyed and followed them till they entered the hot water of the ford. But the flames on the water's surface frightened him, and he went no further.

'The next morning he continued his journey, and in due course returned to the capital of Vikramaditya. Having gladdened his parents with his now impeccable learning, he then went to see the gallant monarch, to whom he displayed his knowledge with great enthusiasm. Courteously questioned by the king, he recounted his tale from the beginning, including the marvel he had seen in the Andhra country.

'The king was curious. He went there himself, and saw the temple and the blazing waters before it. Spending the night at the temple, he also witnessed the dances and all the rites performed by the divine damsels. "Come with us," they said to him as they departed in the morning, and he boldly went behind them to the bubbling source of the water. Such was the heat which arose from its waves that even the birds in the sky did not want to fly across it, what to say of other creatures.

'Smiling with suppressed amusement, the nymphs cast meaningful glances at Vikramaditya as they dived into the ford. Following them the king too leapt into the burning water. As he entered its inner recess the eight beauties happily took him by the hand and led him to their city.'

'The place was adorned with banners and gates of gold with many jewelled columns. The nymphs took the king into their mansion and seated him on a gem-studded throne. They washed his feet and welcomed him with lighted lamps and performed other appropriate ceremonies. As he sat upon the fine throne, one nymph tempted him with clever words: "O King, even Indra and the others have wanted us but, knowing you to be the epitome of manliness, we would like to have only Your Majesty as our master. We are the eight magic powers. This power is named Aṇimā or minuteness, which attribute she harbours in the slenderness of her waist. She wishes to wed you. So does she, named Mahimā or vastness, who cleverly bears this glory in her ample hips. Look at Laghimā or lightness, with whose favour a man may move about in the sky without support, as if by magic. And this power is Garimā or weightiness, bearing this quality in her breasts; she has fallen in love with you who carry such weight in the world. This is Prāpti or possession, who is here to be possessed by you, the repository of all valour. To have her is to have everything. Here to serve you, O King, is Iśitā or supremacy, by whose favour a man is able to do and to undo all things, and also to change them. And in your service too is Vaśitā or mastery, a single glance from whom gives one dominion over this whole world of gods, demons and humans. Enjoy finally this power named Prākāmyā, or irresistible will. She enables the attainment of desired objects in all, conditions, and herself desires you. Other capabilities, like that of entering another's body, are the servants of the eight great magic powers. Attended by them, O King, rule this realm unhampered, as you deem proper."

'After listening to the nymph, King Vikramaditya replied with a smile lighting up his face: "What you say is true, and I am very pleased. Everyone gets satisfaction from success in doing something. But I did not come here to gain this kingdom or your magic powers. I came simply to see this marvel. So grant me your grace, and do not be offended if I do not act as you wish."

'Observing that the noble king had decided not to stay, the nymphs gave him eight jewels which would enable him to attain their powers. As for Vikrama, he took leave from them and came out of the boiling lake.

'As the king proceeded to Ujjayini he saw on the way a brahmin gone grey with age, tottering along with a staff for support, "Old age has enfeebled you, brahmin," he asked kindly, "where do you want to go?" The dotard explained why he was on the road. "I am called Vishnu Śarmā," he said. "I am from the Kaśyapa family and live in Kanchīpura. I have always been plagued by bad luck. My wife is old, ill-tempered and sharp-tongued. She has many children and frequently scolds me for my poverty. 'A curse on this life, you fool!' she says, 'you are no good at work and always in trouble. Your indigence is unending. From the time you married me to this day, my clothes have been in tatters and my life has been spent in misery. My limbs are twisted from always sleeping on the ground. There is nothing for my comfort, nor enough food for my stomach. A man without money is like one dead. Even his relatives are unwilling to keep him company, and they go away. A woman who gets a husband devoid of learning, discrimination and money is spurned by her kinsfolk. It is better for a girl to lose her husband in youth, rather than be derided aṣ the wife of a pauper.' These harsh words of my wife pierced me like arrows, and so I set out to gain wealth or perish in the process. But to behold you at the break of day is like attaining the eight magic powers. I will certainly gain some benefit from you beyond my imagination.'"

'After listening to the old man, the king reflected: "Alas, poverty leads to humiliation, even at the hands of one's wife. As it is said:

'My beauty, won't you do something nice for me?'
'Why don't you do it yourself?'
'Shame on your temper!'
'And who provokes one with nasty words,
more than you?'
'Curse you for answering back at every word!'
'Curse your father!'
Can there be any happiness for a couple who thus

keep sniping and quarrelling with each other all the time?

'"How strange are men's actions," the king thought,

Some people help many others,
some help only themselves,
and some cannot do even that.
Such is the ultimate fruit
of good and evil deeds."

'His heart moved by pity and compassion, the king then gave the eight jewels to the brahmin.'

After recounting this story, the statuette said to King Bhoja: 'Sit upon this throne if you have such fortitude and magnanimity, O King!' But the king heard her and kept silent.

22. The Elixir of Kāmākshā

Once again King Bhoja was curious to hear the narrative. 'Tell me a tale,' he said to the statuette. And she told him one with smiling glances which delighted the hearts of his assembled courtiers. 'Your eagerness for a story gives me eloquence, O King,' she said, 'do not disdain me as just a wooden puppet, but pay attention.

'King Vikramaditya travelled the world to see its marvels, with just his sword as a companion. Fatigued by the blazing sun, he once came to a forest looking for a place to rest. At that time a certain brahmin also arrived and sat down near the king. "From where have you come, brahmin?" the king asked. "I am a pilgrim on a trip around the world," the brahmin replied, "and you, sir, where are you coming from?" "I am a pilgrim like you, sir," the king responded. But the brahmin looked at him carefully and said: "My lord, who are you? Your appearance denotes majesty and displays all the signs of royalty. You merit a throne. Why are you travelling thus?"

'Pressed for an answer, the king said: "I am the kshatriya Vikramaditya. I come from the city of Ujjayini. But my purpose, you should know, is only amusement." At these words the brahmin's hair bristled with joy, his head shook and his hands trembled, as he recalled the king's unequalled splendour. "Where are your fan bearers and your tent carriers?" he asked eagerly. "Where is the royal parasol, bright as the enchanting moon of autumn? Where today do you rest your noble feet, caressed by the jewelled diadems of vassal lords? And in what harem, proud of its divine women of enchanting beauty and loveliness, do you repose here, O King? People like me are incapable of enjoying pleasures even if they could accumulate them, but why have you given up for nothing the earthly delights you have?"

'"This is my way, brahmin," the king replied with a laugh, "who can change one's nature? But why do you look as if you are very tired?" The brahmin answered: "What can I say about why I am exhausted? I am suffering terribly." "Tell me the cause," asked the king. "Listen then, Your Majesty," the brahmin said. "On the hill of Mahānīla abides the goddess Kāmākshā. There is a cave in front of her temple. Its portals open only with the password of her incantation. Inside it is a tank of ripened elixir. I went there and spent twelve years reciting the incantation, but the door of the cave did not open. That is why I am so tired and depressed."

'"Show me that place," said the king, "I will try to do something." The brahmin conducted him to the site, and they both spent the night there. As they slept, the goddess came to the king in a dream and said: "Why have you come here, O King? This door will open only if a man with the thirty-two auspicious marks is sacrificed here, and not otherwise."

'The king left the brahmin sleeping and went at dawn to the door of the cave. In the absence of any other man with the auspicious marks, as he was about to cut off his own head, the goddess held his hand. "O crown jewel of heroes!" she said, "I am satisfied. Ask for a boon." "If you are pleased," said the king, "give this man the ripened elixir." Kāmākshā then opened the cave and gave the elixir to the brahmin, whose heart's desire was thus fulfilled by the great deed of Vikramaditya; and the king returned to Ujjayinī.'

After listening to the statuette's tale, King Bhoja turned back from the throne.

23. The King's Daily Schedule

A statuette told the king the twenty-third tale when he
came once again to ascend the throne.

'The noble King Vikrama ruled an empire from his
capital in Avanti,' the statuette said. 'His fame had spread
in all directions, and the glow of crown jewels from thirty-
six royal houses lit his feet.

'In the sacred moment preceding dawn the king would
awaken to the auspicious sounds of the kettledrum and
the conch shell, and the chanting of his bards. Arising
from his bed, he would move to a comfortable seat where
he would meditate on the Supreme Spirit and reflect on
his lineage, his duties and his vows. At the end of the
morning rites he would make a ritual gift of gold and set
his feet on the ground.

'The king would then take exercise by practising with
the thirty-six weapons, and have his body massaged in the
rubbing room. After bathing in royal style in the pavilion
of the pool, he would put on fresh laundered clothes and
offer prayers to the supreme and primeval Lord. Thereafter
all his limbs would be embellished with jewels and
decorations in the hall of ornaments, and he would take
his seat upon the lion throne in the royal assembly. There,
attended by his prime minister, commander-in-chief,
ministers, courtiers, nobles and family, he would transact
the business of state.

'At midday the hour would be announced with the
beating of drums. The king would then perform the noon
prayers and provide for charity to the poor, the helpless
and the afflicted. After this he would dine, surrounded by
his kinsfolk, friends and attendants, on food seasoned with
all the six flavours, ending the repast with a betel leaf
dressed with camphor water.

'Anointing his body with fragrances of sandalwood,
saffron, aloe and musk, the king would then sleep for a

short while on a golden bed with a mattress of swansdown and pillows on either side. He would lie on his left side, for,

> To sit after eating makes one fat;
> to lie outstretched gives strength;
> and to lie on the left side aids
> longevity. But to run after eating
> is to have death running after you.

'On getting up, the king would partake of worldly pleasures: some moments in amusement with his parakeets, mynas, swans and other birds; some others in dalliance with charming women adept in all kinds of clever talk; and yet others in entertainment by dancing girls. The evening would find him in the royal assembly hall, fanned by maidens with tinkling bracelets, the white parasol held over his head. There, surrounded by thirty-six court entertainers, he granted audiences appropriate for the evening.

'After performing the evening prayers and other rites, the king would retire to sleep, his mind purified with meditation on the gods and the gurus. Thus did he spend his time, partaking of all the delights of this world.

'Once, having spent the night in many and varied pleasures, the king told his ministers: "I had a dream last night. It was in the last watch but one, as I slept with the women of my harem. The room was bright with jewel lamps. I dreamt that I was smeared with a paste of red sandalwood and mounted on a buffalo as dark and enormous as a boulder broken off from the Black Mountain. I was alone and being carried away swiftly towards the south, the direction of which the patron is the god of death. Then I woke up. What could this dream be, and what could it portend?"

'On hearing these words, the ministers and the priests gazed sadly at each other with downcast eyes. For a moment they maintained a discreet silence, as retainers are always afraid to say something unpleasant, even if it is true. "Lord of the earth," they said eventually, "you know the reality of everything. Still, you want an explanation of which you are already aware.

> Riding on a cow, a bull, or an elephant;
> a palace, a mountain peak, or plants;
> weeping and death; being smeared
> with ordure or having sex with someone
> with whom it is forbidden:
> all these are auspicious in dreams.

'"But being mounted on an ass, a buffalo, a bear or an ape is inauspicious. White is good, except in ashes, cotton, cowries and bones. Dark is bad, except in elephants, horses, cattle and brahmins. Thus, riding a buffalo is somewhat unfavourable, Your Majesty. Some gold should be given away to negate this evil dream."

'The king then caused his treasury to be left open for three days, and a proclamation to be made in the city centre: "O people! Anyone may come once and take away whatever he wishes." Thus he gave great bounties for three days to neutralize the evil dream. It is said,

> "How great was Vikrama's charity!
> Merely on account of an evil dream
> he let the people of the city make free
> with his treasury for three days."

'King Bhoja,' said the statuette, 'if you have such munificence as did Vikramaditya, then ascend this throne of great Indra.' But the king was astonished by her words, and went back to his own palace.

24. The Judgement of Śālivāhana

*O*n another occasion, as King Bhoja was again about to ascend the throne after having made all the arrangements for his coronation, the twenty-fourth statuette said to him: 'O King, only a person with the magnanimity of Vikramaditya may sit upon this throne.

'When that king ruled,' the statuette continued, 'the earth was laden with grain, the rivers flowed with milk and curds, and the trees dripped with honey. No one was inclined to wickedness, and none pursued profit or sought pleasure to the exclusion of everything else. Such was the state of the populace under that virtuous king.'

'In Vikramaditya's kingdom there was a city called Purandarapuri. In it there lived an extremely rich merchant who had four sons. In course of time this vaiśya¹ grew old and ill. As he neared death, he summoned his four sons and said: "O my sons, when I am gone, the four of you are bound to have disputes irrespective of whether you stay together or not. So, while I am still alive, I have divided my wealth among you four, beginning with the eldest. The four shares are buried under the four posts of this bed. You should take them in that order, from the eldest to the youngest." To this the sons agreed.

'After the merchant's demise the four brothers stayed together for a month, but then their wives began to quarrel. "Why have an altercation?" they thought. "Our father had already made out four shares while he was still alive. We should take the apportioned wealth which is under his bed, and live separately in peace."

'Having agreed to this, when they dug beneath the bed four copper caskets emerged from under its four posts. One had some earth inside it, and the other three contained charcoal, bones, and straw respectively. The four brothers were mystified. "Our father made a fine division," they said, "but who can understand the method in this?" They went to the local council and explained the situation, but the councillors too were unable to understand the rationale of the division.

'Thereafter the four brothers went wherever there were knowledgeable people in the city and explained the matter, but no one could come to a decision. They went once to Ujjayini and narrated the tale of the division before the royal assembly. After listening to them the king immediately instructed his ministers to look into their case. "Your father was a man of discrimination," the ministers told them after considering the matter. "If he set aside straw, coal and the other things, it was not without purpose. But this has to be judged by people of spiritual eminence."

'Thus advised, the vaiśyas carried on. They met with ridicule at every village and town they visited. Eventually they came to the city of Pratishthāna, and spoke before its leaders who also were unable to make a pronouncement. At that time Śālivāhana lived in a potter's house in the city. Having heard of this matter, he went to the city fathers and said to them: "Gentlemen, what is so difficult to understand in this? What is so surprising? How is it that you do not perceive the method in this division?" "Young man," they replied, "this is a mystery to us. We do not understand it. If you do, then tell us what this manner of division means."

'Śālivāhana said: "These four are the sons of the same rich man. During his lifetime itself their father made an apportionment among them, from the eldest to the youngest. To the eldest he gave earth: that means all the lands that he had acquired. To the second he gave straw, which means all his grain. To the third he gave bones, which indicates all his cattle. And he gave charcoal to the fourth, which denotes all his gold." Thus did Śālivāhana determine the shares between the brothers, and they returned home, satisfied with the decision.

'King Vikrama also heard the news about this determination of the shares, and marvelled greatly. To learn more he sent a letter to the city of Pratishthāna. "Greetings," he wrote, "to the illustrious city fathers of Pratishthāna, who are ever engaged in the six sacred duties of praying, conducting prayers, studying, teaching, giving and receiving ritual gifts; and who are devoted to the virtues of observance, abstinence and other rules of conduct. After enquiring about their welfare, King Vikrama says: the person in your locality who made the decision on the quadruple division should be despatched to be presented before us."

'After seeing this letter, the city fathers called Śālivāhana and told him: "Śālivāhana, you have been summoned to Ujjayini by King Vikrama, the king of kings, the supreme lord at whose feet other kings pay homage, and who is a wish-fulfilling tree for all supplicants. You must go there."

'"Who is King Vikrama?" said Śālivāhana. "I will not go on his summons. I have nothing to do with him. If he has any business with me, let him come himself." The civic leaders then sent a letter to the king, saying that Śālivāhana was not prepared to go.

'At the letter's contents the king's face flushed with anger. He set out with a force of eighteen legions and, on arrival at Pratishthāna, surrounded it and sent messengers to Śālivāhana. "King Vikrama, the king of all kings, summons you, Śālivāhana," they said. "Come to see him." But Śālivāhana replied: "O messengers, I will not go all alone to see the king. I will see Vikrama with a fourfold army, on the field of battle. Convey this to the king."

'The messengers reported this to the king, who proceeded to the battle field for the contest. As for Śālivāhana, he took clay in the potter's house and crafted with it a force of elephants, chariots, cavalry and infantry. Bringing it to life with an incantation, he came out of the

city with this fourfold army and went forth into the field.
As the two forces marched out,

> The horizon shook and the ocean
> rocked with fear; the mountains trembled
> and the serpent king quaked in the nether world;
> the earth rolled and mighty snakes
> furiously spewed venom. All this happened
> many times as the king's army went forth.
>
> The glorious armies glittered
> with endless troops of cavalry
> as swift as the wind,
> and masses of rutting elephants;
> the entire sky was covered
> with flags, whisks and banners;
> and the three worlds were filled
> with the sound of gongs,
> tabors and kettle drums.

'A mighty battle now took place, and Śālivāhana's
army was destroyed by Vikramaditya.[2] Much distraught,
Śālivāhana recalled the boon given to him by his father
to remember the latter in times of trouble. He called in
his mind his parent Śesha, the serpent king, who
promptly despatched all his snakes to provide support.
Bitten by them, the entire force of Vikramaditya was
rendered unconscious by their venom, and fell fainting on
the field.

'The valiant Vikrama longed to revive his army which
was thus disabled, for he was a king devoted to the
protection of his servants. He went to Mount Mandara and
worked single-mindedly on propitiating Vāsuki, the chief
of the eight serpent tribes, Taking the jar of nectar given
by that adversary, he then turned back, anxious to
resuscitate his army.

'On the way he saw two brahmins, who matched the Aśvinas in beauty, the sun and the moon in glory, the Marutas in majesty, and the two Paulastya lords in splendour.[3] Raising their right hands, these two supposed brahmins blessed the king with future happiness, and said: "You are compassionate to the poor, O King. The prayers of supplicants bear fruit only through you. Great givers like Dadhichi, Śibi, Jīmūtavāhana and Angeśvara[4] have been outstripped and forgotten because of your largesse. You brought Bāli's elixir and essence from the nether world[5] and comforted two brahmins with them. There is nothing which magnanimous people like you cannot give up. You obtained the quilt, the crayon and the magic staff from Trikāla Nātha in the Himalaya,[6] and gave them away to a king exiled from his kingdom. Your Majesty's famous, marvellous and extraordinary deeds cannot be described adequately even by the thousand-mouthed Śesha, what to say of any one else."

'The king was pleased with their pleasant words. "Choose what you desire, you two," he said. The brahmins then told him: "Your Majesty is always striving only to help others. Give us this jar full of nectar, O King. Do not take back your words, for a promise once made must be kept."

'The brahmins spoke with the insistence of pent-up excitement, and the king reflected on their words. "Who are you two?" he asked. "Know us to be the servants," they replied, "of Śesha, on whom rests the god Vishnu, and on even one of whose heads this world would be no more than a mustard seed. You, O King, intend to kill his own son and are here after obtaining nectar from the propitiated Vāsuki. Therefore we approached you. Śesha sent us, knowing your goodness and your incomparable heart. 'Children,' he told us, 'beg King Vikramaditya for the nectar. He is kind to brahmins and will not want to refuse your request.' So now do what you think proper."

'The two serpent youths disguised as brahmins had spoken with candour. After listening to them the king thought for a moment. If Vikramaditya did not give the gift which two brahmins begged him," he said to himself. "the ignominy of this will be impossible to erase. So, let dharma prosper, even though the designs of my enemies prosper with it. I will give them the nectar even though I earned it by penance." And the king gave away the nectar to the two false brahmins. They praised him and returned to their own abode, while he went back to Ujjayini.

'The serpent Vāsuki was pleased with Vikrama's heroic conduct, and immediately revived his army,' the statuette continued, 'he also praised the noble king. If there is anyone on this earth capable of doing what he did, that person alone would be worthy of ascending this royal throne.'

After listening to the story told by the statuette, King Bhoja returned home, thinking that Vikramaditya was indeed divine.

25. The Halting of Saturn

A statuette restrained the king with appropriate words when he was once again inclined to ascend the throne. 'King Bhoja,' she said, 'listen to the tale I will tell you today, and then decide, after understanding it, what is proper for you to do here.'

'When Vikramaditya was king, once an astrologer who had knowledge of the four hundred thousand celestial bodies came to the royal assembly. Presented by the chamberlain, he pronounced a blessing for the king and took a suitable seat.'

'"What are all the arts you know?" asked the king. "Your Majesty," the astrologer replied, "I know the shape of the past, the future and the present. I do so through the movements of the sun and the moon, the planets and the starry constellations; through their rising and setting, eclipses and accelerations, situations and aspects, friendly and adverse natures, strengths and weaknesses; and also through the eight types of omens, like celestial and aerial portents, and terrestrial features, sounds, signs and prodigies."

'The king wished to know about the future, and on his enquiry the astrologer said: "Your Majesty, there will be a famine here which will last twelve years." "Sir!" cried the king on hearing this, "there is no transgression of proper governance in my kingdom. Nor is there any propagation of wrong policies. The people are not oppressed. There is no animosity towards religion or interference in pious works; no altercation with the helpless or persecution of the defenceless; no slandering of others or teaching of falsehood. None are inclined to wickedness. No tax is levied on those who should not be taxed. Neither is there any destruction of sacred images, or affliction of sages, or departure from the rules of caste. How then can a famine be possible here?"

'"O King," the soothsayer replied, "if Saturn pierces the cart shaped constellation of Rohiṇī, and moves into the house of Mars or Venus, then there is a famine for twelve years. As Varāhamihira[1] has said:

The clouds for certain will not rain
for twelve years if Saturn, Mars and Venus
penetrate and pass through the cart of Rohiṇī."

'After hearing this, the king initiated religious works like charities, holy practices, fire sacrifices and other propitiatory and auspicious rites for the sake of the populace. But it did not rain.

'The king was deeply distressed at the sufferings of his people. "If the head of a family sees his family suffering," he said to himself, "and does not care for it as much as he can, it is sinful of him. If the head of a village does not care for the suffering villagers, it is sinful too. And if the lord of a country levies taxes on it, but does not protect it when it suffers, it is indeed a sin for him."

'At a loss for what to do, the king was sick at heart. "I have prayed to the goddess who fulfills wishes," he thought. "I have sacrificed in different fires, and propitiated the planets with the best ceremonies. But for some reason the heaven still does not rain upon the earth." As the king worried thus, a disembodied voice was heard: "Stop worrying, O King. You are the first among noble-minded men. As you alone have satisfied the wish-fulfilling goddess, she is pleased to give you a divine chariot filled with celestial weapons, which can go everywhere. Mount it swiftly, O hero, and go for the cart of Rohiṇī, your bow drawn and the divine missiles blazing irresistibly. Then halt the crooked course of Saturn!"

'Urged by the voice, the king interrupted the course of Saturn with the power of divine weapons, like Daśaratha[2] in days gone by. Extremely pleased with Vikramaditya's heroism, Saturn gave him the boon that there would be no drought in his land. After receiving this gift, the king descended and returned to the city. Thus it is that even today there is generally no famine in the Mālava country.

'Adorn this fair throne if you are capable of acting similarly,' said the statuette. The king's desire was thwarted by these words from the figurine, and he went back to the inner apartment, his face averted.

26. The Heavenly Cow

*O*nce again the cultivated voice of a statuette rang out as King Bhoja came forward to ascend the throne: 'O King, this is *his* throne! Sit upon it if you can manifest the heroism, the generosity and the fortitude which *he* had.' And when the king eagerly asked her to tell him a story, she recounted one of the deeds of Vikramaditya.

'There was never a king like Vikramaditya for qualities such as heroism, magnanimity, compassion, discrimination and fortitude,' the statuette said. 'What is more, he did what he said. And he said what was in his heart. Whatever followed from his words, he would do. For he was a good man. It is said,

As they think, so they speak.
As they speak, so they do.
In good men there is uniformity
in their thought, speech and action.

To help, to speak kindly, and to have
great affection is in the nature
of good men. Does anyone
have to make the moon cool?

'Once Indra sat upon his throne in the city of the immortal gods. He was attended by many divine princes and sages, and countless categories of deities; by his minister, the moon god; and by Viśvavasu and other chiefs of the demigods. Also present were the celestial nymphs Ghritāchī, Menakā, Rambhā, Sahajanyā, Tilottamā, Urvaśī and Sukeśī, together with Priyadarśanā; the eight Magic Powers and the presiding deities of the eight directions. All of them had come to pay homage at great Indra's noble feet.

'In the course of a discussion in that great assembly, the sage Nārada and others who stood there praised men of merit. "No king can surpass Vikramaditya in virtue," Nārada said to Indra. "Endowed with nobility and courage, possessed of magnanimity and fortitude, he alone protects the people of the world, his valour unstained." Indra marvelled at these words. Seeing Surabhi, the heavenly cow which grants wishes, nearby, he told her to go and find out about the virtues of Vikramaditya.

'On receiving great Indra's commandment, Surabhi proceeded to the earth and fell into a nasty pit where she floundered like a common cow. At that time the king was on his way back to the city after touring the provinces in disguise. He heard the distressed bovine cries and wondered: "From where comes this cry, like that of a cow, in this forest full of carnivorous beasts? I must look into this." And getting to that place, he saw a miserable cow with eyes streaming tears, feebly trying to climb out of the pit into which she had fallen.

'The king was filled with compassion. "No one is as foolish," he said to himself, "as one who has the power, but does not do his master's work or help a friend in trouble; or rescue the helpless, keep his word, grant favours sought, and help others." Thinking thus, the hero caught hold of the cow's tail at the root. But he could not pull her out as she was too heavy.

'Meanwhile the sun set and at night it began to rain. Despite this, the king stayed there, guarding the helpless cow. He covered her with his own garments, and himself remained naked. In the morning he made another strong effort to extricate her, but she would not move. At this moment a great tiger burst upon them with a loud roar, its tail bolt upright like a staff and its limbs contracted for a spring.

'Seeing this ferocious beast draw near, the king fearlessly came between it and the cow whose eyes rolled in terror. Within moments, the hungry tiger raised its feet and leapt with gaping jaws upon the cow, falling on her like a mountain. With a terrible roar it also dealt the king a thunderous blow with its sharp-nailed paw. The blow was hard to bear, but the king withstood it and struck the predator with his sword, which flashed like lightning. Thus he warded off the furious attacks of the tiger as it tried to get at the cow.

'The cow had observed the king's compassion, resoluteness and other qualities. She now got up by herself and said: "O King, I am Surabhi, the wish-fulfilling cow. I came from heaven to investigate your compassion and other virtues. Their proof I have now seen. There is no king on earth as compassionate as you. I am very pleased. Choose a boon."

'"By your grace, I lack nothing," replied the king. "What can I ask for?" The cow was amazed at his selfless and steadfast words. "I am yours," she said simply, and the king proceeded with her to his capital.

'As he travelled with the cow on the highway, a brahmin came up and offered a benediction. "O King,' he said, "poverty has made me a magician. For I can see everyone, but no one at all sees me. It is said,

> Poverty, I salute you. Through
> your grace I have become a magician.
> For I can see the world, but none see me."

'"What are you asking for, brahmin?" said the King. "O King," the brahmin replied, "Your Majesty is a wishing tree for supplicants. Do whatever will remove my poverty for as long as I live." "Then this wish-fulfilling cow will grant your desires," the king said. "Take her." And he gave him the cow.

'The brahmin took the cow and went home, feeling as if he had gained the joys of paradise. The king returned to his capital. And Surabhi the cow returned to heaven after giving the brahmin all that he wished for.

'If there is anyone greater than Vikramaditya in acts of such marvellous generosity, then name him, King Bhoja!' the statuette concluded. 'Anyone else is unworthy of this throne of Indra. So cease to hanker for it, King Bhoja, and be content.'

27. The Gambler

*W*hen the king again arrived to mount the throne, a statuette supporting it addressed him: 'Lord of Bhoja, ascend this great throne of mighty Indra only if you have Vikrama's quality of helping others everywhere.' 'Tell me, you who speak so sweetly,' asked the king, 'what was this quality and the nature of his compassion? I am all ears.' Urged thus, she told him the twenty-seventh story of Vikramaditya, who was always inclined to help others.

'While travelling the earth, alone and in disguise, King Vikramaditya once came to a ·city called Chandravati. "I will stay here for five days," he said to himself, and he went to a most beautiful temple where he saluted the deity and took a seat in the congregation hall.

'After some time another man arrived there. He was handsomely attired, like a prince. His garments were of silk and he wore all manners of ornaments. His body had been rubbed with a pomade of sandalwood, perfumed with camphor, saffron, aloe and musk. Accompanying him were some courtesans, with whom he amused himself in flirtatious tale-telling and conversation before going out with them again. The king observed him, and wondered who he could be.

'The same man came again the following day. This time he was alone, without his robes and ornaments, and clad merely in a loincloth. Looking miserable, he flung himself on the floor of the temple hall.

'The king saw this now wretched man sitting and sighing not far from him and, as if to soothe his suffering, asked kindly: "Good sir, you came here yesterday sporting a splendid dress. Today you are in this condition. What is the reason?"

'"O master," the man replied, "why do you speak thus? Yesterday I was in another condition. Now I am in this. It is because of destiny. Thus,

The bees which flourished on ichor
from the rutting elephant's temple,
their limbs perfumed by the pollen
of the blooming lotus, now daily
while their time on the bitter foliage
of the lime and the sunflower."

'"Who are you, sir?" asked the king. "I am a gambler," the man replied. "Do you understand the game of dice?" the king asked further. The man said: "On that subject I am certainly an expert. I am always there with the gamesters, playing the dice day and night. I know the game gatāgatam or 'go and come', and am a master at making wagérs. I know too the power of the mind in setting impregnable defences with elephants, knights, ministers and chariots in the four-limbed game of chess. I am skilled in winning money, and have defeated even clever players. But, though always capable, I was beaten today by destiny and reduced to this condition. So, I wander, stricken by fate. That is the supreme power in the world. What man can do is meaningless. One's efforts are futile when one ignores this fact."

'"Whoever you may be, sir," said the king, "you are very intelligent. Why have you devoted yourself to this extremely wicked pursuit of gaming?" "What does not even an intelligent man do when driven by his karma?" the gambler replied. "And it is said,

Driven by his own karma,
what can the intelligent man do?
The minds of men have
always followed their karma."

'"Gentle sir," said the king, "gambling is the root of great evils. The game of dice is the repository of all vices. It is said,

What man of clear mind
will engage in the pursuit
of gaming? It is the home
of ill fame, and the abode
of thieves and harlots.
It is the king of vices,
and the first of the
dangerous roads to hell.

'"There are seven very evil vices which intelligent people
eschew," the king continued, "it is said,

Gambling, meat eating, wine drinking,
fornicating, hunting, theft, and adultery
are seven very evil vices
which intelligent people should eschew.

'"Moreover,

Yudhishthira was brought down by gambling,
the ogre Baka by eating meat,
Balarāma by drinking wine,
Indra by fornication,
King Brahamadatta by hunting,
Yayāti by theft
and the great
ten-headed Rāvaṇa by adultery.
People can be ruined
by even one of these vices.
Who will not be destroyed by all?

'"Therefore, my friend, do not play dice any more and
destroy your self-respect and your wealth, virtue and prestige.
This is what has brought you to your present condition."
    '"You do not know the pleasure of dicing," the gambler
replied. "Nectar is but a name. Food can cause illness.

Ornaments merely satisfy vanity. The pleasure of women turns sour because one cannot trust them. That of music, song and dance depends on others. And spiritual bliss is unattainable. Thus, gambling gives the one definite pleasure in this transient world. Even yogis pray to be absorbed in it. Thus,

As the gambler meditates on his stake,
the separated lover on his beloved,
and the skilled archer on his target,
so may I mediate on you, O Lord."

'"Alas," thought the king on hearing these words,

"Ignorance is indeed worse than anger
and all the other vices. Blinded by it,
man cannot tell the good from the bad."

'The king then gave further instruction to the gambler. "If you really want to help others," said the latter, "then do one thing for me." "I will do it if you give up this vice of gambling," said the king. "So be it," the gambler said. "But do not tell me to stop. Do me a favour, if you are my friend. Whether this game of dice causes happiness or grief, I am not inclined to give it up. So, do not forbid it to me. But, since you have treated me as a friend, I am in your hands. Act like one and solve my problem. But even a friend cannot provide success only through instruction. Be my support by giving me some money." The king smiled and said: "I will do what is proper." Then he kept silent.

'By this time, two brahmins from a foreign land had arrived and sat down in another part of the temple. They were conferring amongst themselves, and one said: "I have seen all the works written in the goblin tongue. In them it is said that to the north-east of this temple, at a distance of five bow shots, there are located three jars full of dīnāra coins. Near them is an image of the deity Bhairava, and they can be obtained by sprinkling that image with one's own blood."

'The king heard this conversation. He went to the place talked about and sprinkled the image of Bhairava with the blood of his own body. "O King," the contented deity said to him, "I am pleased. Choose a boon." "If you are pleased," replied the king, "then give the three jars full of dīnāras to this gambler." Bhairava gave him the money, and the gambler went home, praising the king. King Vikrama also returned to his capital.'

Thus did the statuette relate this famous story to King Bhoja, who once more abandoned his desire for mounting the throne.

28. The King stops Human Sacrifice

*A*nother statuette spoke out when the king again attempted to sit on the throne: 'O Monarch! No one is worthy of mounting this throne except one who has the magnanimity and the other virtues of Vikrama.'

'Tell me about his magnanimity and the rest,' said Bhoja. The statue then replied: 'Listen, O King!'

'Once King Vikramaditya went out on a tour and came to a certain city. A clear stream flowed nearby. On its bank was a grove resplendent with many kinds of flowers and fruit, in the middle of which stood a charming temple.

'The king bathed in the stream, offered his prayers, and sat down in the temple. After some time four strangers arrived and also sat near him. "Hello, from where have you come?" asked the king. "We have come from the eastern country," one of them replied.

'"Did you see any new sights in that country?" the king asked. "Master, we saw something extraordinary," said one of the newcomers, "so much so that we barely escaped with our lives."

'"And what was that?" asked the king. The newcomer said: "In that country there is a place called Vetālapurī or Vampire City, where dwells a goddess known as Śoṇitapriyā or Lover of Blood. The people and the ruler of that place offer a human sacrifice to her once a year for the fulfilment of their wishes. Should a stranger happen to be there on the particular day, they kill and offer him like a beast before the goddess. We chanced to be in that city on that very day because of our travels, and the people there came out to finish us off. But by then we had heard about them. We fled and came here, barely escaping with our lives."

'After hearing this account, King Vikrama went to that city and beheld the awesome temple there. Making obeisance to the goddess, he sang a hymn:

"May the holy mothers[1] protect me:
Brahmāṇī, whose face is pure and gentle
like the moon; Maheśvari with her magic charm;
Kaumari, destroyer of the enemy's pride;
Vaishṇavi, who wields the discus;
Varāhi, of the thunderous roar;
Aindri, armed with the thunderbolt;
and Chamuṇḍā, accompanied
by Ganeśa and Rudra."

'Then he sat down in the temple's assembly hall. At that moment a miserable-looking man appeared along with a crowd of people preceded by music. Seeing them, the king said to himself: "This must be the one whom the people have brought here for sacrificing to the goddess. That is why he looks so wretched. I must free him, and proffer myself instead. This body may last for a hundred years, but eventually it must perish. What is worth earning is holy merit and spotless fame. It is said:

Transient is prosperity; youth,
this body, and life itself are fleeting;
transitory is all worldly existence.
Dharma and glory alone are abiding.

'"And further,

This body is but temporary.
Affluence does not last for ever.
Death is ever imminent.
What one should do is
to accumulate holy merit.

'"Furthermore,

Wealth is as dust upon the feet;
youth, is as the torrent

of a mountain stream;
trembling like a drop of water
is the human condition;
and life itself is as foam.

Dharma lifts the bar to heaven's gate.
One who does not follow it
will burn in the fire of grief
when he is struck by remorse
and overcome by age."

'Having thus reflected, the king addressed those people: "Where are you taking this poor man?"

'"We are going to sacrifice him to the goddess," they replied. "Why?" he asked. They said: "The goddess will be pleased with our offering of this man. She will then fulfil our desires."

'"O you people!" said the king, "this man is so puny, and terrified to boot. What satisfaction will the goddess get from the sacrifice of his person? So, let him go. I offer myself instead. My limbs are stout and strong, and the goddess will be content with my flesh. Sacrifice me to her."

'With these words Vikramaditya freed the victim and, going up to the goddess, put his sword to his own throat. At that the deity caught hold of the sword and said: "Mighty hero, I am deeply satisfied with your steadfastness and wish to help others. Choose a boon."

'"Goddess!" prayed the king, "if you are pleased with me, then renounce the sacrifice of human flesh from now." "So be it," the goddess said, and the people cried: "O King, you are indeed like a great tree. You do not seek comfort for yourself, but bear tribulations for the sake of others. Thus,

The tree suffers the sharp summer heat
upon its head, but with its shade

it gives comfort to those
who seek shelter under it.
This is your nature too.
Unmindful of your own ease,
you endure pains every day
for the sake of the people."[2]

'And the king took leave of them, and returned to his own city.'

After recounting this story, the statuette told King Bhoja: 'Your Majesty, sit on this throne if you too have such fortitude and magnanimity.' But the king heard her and remained silent.

29. The Chiromancer

*O*n another occasion, as King Bhoja was about to ascend the throne after making all the arrangements for his coronation, the twenty-ninth statuette spoke to him: 'O King, only that person may sit on this throne who has the magnanimity of Vikramaditya.'

'"And what was that like?" asked the king. The statuette said: 'The noble King Vikrama ruled an empire from the city of Avanti. Once a man learned in the science of chiromancy came there. He knew how to tell the past, the present and the future, and the auspicious and inauspicious portents, from the bodily marks of men and women. In the outskirts of Avanti he was wonderstruck to see a man's footprint marked with the lotus sign.'

'"Is this the footprint of some king?" the chiromancer wondered. "But how can he be travelling alone and on foot? Let me go ahead and see." Proceeding further, he saw a porter with a load of wood on his head. "Alas!" he said, downcast, "with such a mark, if this man is merely a wood-carrier, then my attempt to study the science of chiromancy has been fruitless. What is the point of going to Avanti? I will go back."

'After stopping for some time, the chiromancer thought again: "Since I have come this far, I will carry on to the capital and see what Vikramaditya is like." So he went to Avanti and saw Vikrama in the assembly hall.

'After seeing the king, the diviner was seized with a deep despair. The king was good at reading faces, and realized that the man was distressed. "O stranger," he asked, "how is it that you have become dejected on coming here?" "Sire," the man replied, "on the road I saw a man bearing all the marks of a king, but he was a mere porter with a load of wood. Here I see you, who rule an empire stretching to the sea, but the marks on your body are entirely unfavourable. I am therefore dismayed at the inconsistencies of my science."

'"O scholar," the king then said, "generally sciences cover both rules and exceptions. You should consider carefully what is the rule and what is the exception in this case." The chiromancer marvelled at his words. "How deep is the king's understanding," he reflected, "and how sweet is his speech and powerful his comprehension!" Recapitulating all chiromancy in essence, he said: "O King, this science describes in general numerous attributes of men and women, denoting both favourable and unfavourable portents. But this is the exception: even if there is every auspicious mark on a person's body, they are all rendered invalid should there be a mark like a crow's foot on the palate."

'On hearing this the king had the wood-carrier brought to the assembly. A cake of cornmeal was placed on his palate, and this established a crow's foot there. "Is there any other exception?" the king asked. "If someone's body has all the inauspicious marks, they would nevertheless count as favourable if the intestines from that person's left side are spotted," the chiromancer replied. Drawing out his dagger to test this, as the king was about to rip open the left side of his own abdomen, the chiromancer restrained his hand. "Do not be so audacious, O King," he said. "The intestines inside your belly are bound to be spotted, otherwise how could you have such fortitude and heroic courage? For,

> Wealth is reflected in one's bones,
> happiness in the flesh,
> indulgence in the skin,
> travel in the gait, and
> authority in one's voice.
> But all depends on heroic courage."

'Thus, O King,' the statuette concluded, 'if you have such heroism and fortitude, then you may sit on this throne.'

30. The Magician's Reward

*T*he thirtieth ancient statuette addressed Bhoja when he came again to ascend the excellent throne. 'O King,' she said, 'sit on this throne if you have the generosity and the other virtues like Vikrama.' 'O statue,' replied the king, 'tell me a tale of his generosity.'

'Listen, Majesty,' said the statuette. 'Once King Vikrama was seated upon the throne, attended by all the nobles and the princes. At that time there came a magician who, after giving him the benediction, "Live for ever!" said, "Sire, you are acquainted with all the arts. Many magicians have come before you and displayed their skills. Be kind enough to view my expertise today." "We do not have time now," the king told him, "it is already time to bathe and to eat. We will see it in the morning."

'The king attended the assembly on the following morning, together with all the nobles who had come to wait on him. As the courtiers smiled, looking at the magician who had presented himself, and wondering what unprecedented artifice he would exhibit, another personage entered the royal council chamber and saluted the king.

'The new arrival was a giant of a man, with a great beard and a radiant face. He carried a sword in his hand, and was accompanied by an extremely attractive woman. Young and beautiful, she was dressed in a garment of Chinese silk decorated with designs, and a scarf fragrant with camphor and betel over her breast. The couple's deportment was in keeping with their class and appearance as they stood before the king.

'"Who are you?" asked the king. "I am a servant of Indra," the man replied. "He cursed me once, so I wander on the earth. This is my wife. A war has now begun between the gods and the demons, O King, and I am going there. Let this lovely girl stay with Your Majesty till I return. A woman is a great treasure that should never be left in anyone's power. But Your Majesty has an immaculate reputation for being a brother to other men's wives, and so I decided to leave her with you. In the spirit of helping others, you must guard my wife with every care."

'The man then departed, flying up into the sky with his weapon, while the magician remained standing and everyone looked on. As he disappeared from view there was a terrible shouting in the sky, "Kill! Kill! Strike! Strike!" and all the people seated in the assembly craned their necks, looking upwards with great curiosity. Within moments the man's bloodstained arm and sword fell from the sky in the middle of the royal assembly hall. "Alas, this hero has been slain by the opposing warriors in the battle!" everyone said. "One of his arms with the sword has fallen here!" And even as the assemblage spoke thus, the head also feel down, followed by the torso.

'The woman had also seen this. "Sire," she cried out to the king, "My husband has been killed by his enemies, fighting on the field of battle. His head, his sword arm, and even his trunk have fallen here. I must go to my beloved before he is claimed by the heavenly nymphs. Please provide me with fire."

'"My girl," the king replied, "why should you burn yourself? I will look after you like my own daughter. Preserve your body." "What is this you say, sire!" she retorted. "My master, for whom this body existed, has been felled in the battle field by enemy warriors. For whom will I preserve it now? Moreover, you should not speak thus. Even mindless people know that a woman follows her husband. Thus,

> Moonlight goes with the moon,
> lightning merges in the cloud,
> and women follow the husband.
> This is admitted even by the mindless."[1]

'She then fell at the king's feet, begging that a fire be provided. He tried to dissuade her many times, but the beauty loved her lord and would not relent. She arranged straightaway a wooden pyre, distributed her personal effects and ornaments to deserving people, and forcefully entered the fire with the body of her beloved.

'While the king was mourning the couple's death, in that very moment the warrior suddenly appeared from somewhere. As before, he was gigantic, radiant of face, and armed with a sword. Coming up to the king, he put round his neck a garland of flowers from the celestial wishing tree, on which bees greedy for pollen were still swarming. He then conveyed a message from Indra, and began to give all kinds of information about the battle.

'The entire assembly was stricken with astonishment at this arrival. The king was amazed. "Your Majesty," said the warrior, "I went from here to heaven. There was a mighty battle there between great Indra and the demons. Many of the latter were killed, and some ran away. At the end of the battle the king of the gods graciously told me: 'Commander, I am seeing you after long. Where were you all this time?' 'I spent all these days on earth on account of the master's curse,' I replied. 'But on learning that the master was going to war with the demons, I came here to be of help.'"

'"Great Indra was very pleased. 'O commander,' he said, 'from now onwards you need not stay on earth. Your curse is ended. I am delighted with you. Take this bracelet of gold, studded with the nine gems.' And taking off the bracelet from his own wrist he placed it himself in my hands. 'Master,' I then told him, 'at the time of coming here I left my wife with Vikramaditya. I will fetch her and return immediately.' So I have come. You are a brother to the wives of other men. Give back my wife, and I will return with her to heaven."

'The king was speechless with amazement. "O King," the warrior said again, "why are you silent?" Those sitting nearby said: "She entered the fire with her husband." "But I am alive!" the man exclaimed, "with whom did she enter the fire? You are the king's servants. You only speak his mind. It is well said about appointed officials,

> "Whether it is lawful or not,
> whatever the king says,
> that his retainers echo,
> word for word."

'The king was totally at a loss for a reply. But, after thinking for a moment the wise Vikramaditya made up his mind and uttered a verse:

> "How clever is the application
> of learning which makes even
> the false appear as true.

'All the courtiers were wonderstruck on hearing the king. "What is this that the master says?" they thought, without understanding its purport. But the warrior said: "Your Majesty, my wife is in your harem. Tell me if I may bring her out." "Bring her," replied the king, and he brought his wife from the inner apartment, and took his place before the monarch who hung his head. Then spoke the magician: "O King! O best of kings and brother to other men's wives! O King Vikrama, wish-fulfiller of all supplicants! Live for ever! I am a magician, and I have displayed to you this feat of the science of magic.

'The king was filled with wonder. At that moment there came his treasurer and said: "Master, the king of Pāndya has sent his tribute to Your Majesty." "What has he sent?" the king asked. "Listen with care, master," said the treasurer,

> Eighty millions of gold,
> ninety-three measures of pearls,

fifty load bearing elephants,
the odour of whose rut attracts
the bees, three hundred horses,
and a hundred slave girls
skilled in all the arts:
this is what the Pāndyan king
has sent for His Majesty,
the illustrious King Vikrama."

'"O treasurer," the king said, "give all this to the magician."
And it was so given.'

After telling this story, the statuette said to King Bhoja:
'Your Majesty, sit on this throne if you have such generosity.'
And the king remained silent.

31. The Genie's Tale

*B*hoja had brought the earth under his supreme sway. Wishing once again to ascend the excellent throne, he approached the thirty-first statuette. 'King Bhoja,' she said, 'you may have the pleasure of mounting this throne only if you possess the daring of Vikramaditya.'

'Tell me, beautiful one, what was his daring like?' the worthy monarch asked. 'Listen, O King,' said the statuette. 'During Vikramaditya's reign a yogi once came to see him in the assembly. He was a digambara, one who goes naked. All his limbs were sprinkled with ash, and on his forehead he bore the triple mark,[1] also in ash. He wore clogs of gemstone on his feet, and looked a veritable Śiva, the repository of all knowledge. The high-minded king marvelled at seeing him, and greeted him with all honours.

'The naked yogi placed a fruit in the king's hands after pronouncing a benediction:

May the Lord Vishnu, devotion to whom
is the price of salvation even as the bridal fee
is for marrying a maiden, fulfill the wishes
of Your Majesty, his devotee.

'Sitting down, he then said: "O King, I am going to perform a fire sacrifice in the great cemetery on the fourteenth day of the dark half, that is the moonless night, of the month of Mārgaśīrsha.[2] Your Majesty is a benefactor of others and the greatest of heroes. So you must be my assistant on this occasion.

'"What will I be required to do?" asked the king. "Not far from the cemetery is a śamī tree," the naked one said, "and on it lives a genie. You will need to bring him to me,[3] maintaining complete silence." The king promised to do this.

'On the fourteenth day of the dark fortnight the ascetic collected the material for the fire sacrifice and took position in the great cemetery. The king also went there at midnight. He was shown the way to the śami tree and, getting to it, he put the corpse possessed by the genie on his shoulder. As he was returning to the cemetery, the genie said: "O King, tell a story to relieve the travail of this journey." But the king said nothing, for he feared he would break the silence. "O ruler," the genie spoke again, "you are not telling a story as you fear to break the silence. So I will recount one instead. At its end, if you do not reply to my question for the same reason even though you know the answer, your head will burst into a thousand pieces." The genie then narrated:

The Balance of Virtue

'On the southern side of the Himalaya is a city called Vindhyavati. There reigned a king named Suvichāra, who had a son, Jayasena. The latter once went to the forest to hunt. Pursuing an elephant he saw there, he entered a dense jungle through which he somehow found the way back to the city. While he was returning alone, he noticed a river in the middle of the forest.

'A brahmin was performing his midday devotions there. The foolish prince addressed him with arrogance: "Brahmin, hold my horse till I drink water and come back. Do it straightaway, right now itself." Spoken to in this way, the brahmin retorted angrily; "Prince, am I your servant to hold your horse? Is it because of ignorance or affluence, pride or youth, or some perversity of princely passion that you speak thus?" The king's son was incensed, and, consumed by the pride of youth, he struck the brahmin with his whip. Smarting under the lash, the noble brahmin went to the palace gate and raised an outcry.

'The king was sitting on the seat of judgement. He called the brahmin and listened to the entire story about his wicked son. Eyes red with anger, he cursed his offspring with many a harsh word, and instructed his minister: "Exile him from the state for assaulting a brahmin. This is an irrevocable order. Carry it out."

'The minister knew his duties and was skilled in executing orders. "Sire," he said on this occasion, "the prince is now competent to bear the burdens of government. Why are you exiling him from the country? This will not be proper." "It is proper, 'minister," said the king. "It will be appropriate because he struck the brahmin's person with a whip. Intelligent people should not incur the enmity of brahmins. It is said,

A wise person does not eat poison,
nor play with serpents.
Nor should he censure yogis
or antagonize brahmins.

'"The old verse from the conversation between Krishna and Yudhishthira[4] in praise of virtuous and charitable conduct is well known:

Bharata, those who are about to lose
their fortunes are hostile to astrologers,
those their lives to physicians,
and those who are going to lose
both fortune and life
are hostile to brahmins.

'"There are many similar sayings in the world. If indulgence is shown to the prince on account of his youth, it will without doubt destroy the family. That is not my wish, and so there is no question but that he must be exiled from the kingdom."

'The king was a stickler for form. Thus commanded by him, the minister stood up and said respectfully: "O protector of the people, you are expelling your only son!

Master, how can you exile the sole pivot of your kingdom? The noble brahmin was tolerant and is satisfied. You too, master, should be tolerant of this single transgression." But the king knew his duties. "In that case, O minister," he said, "the hand with which he struck the brahmin needs to be cut off."

'As this punishment was about to be carried out, the brahmin arrived and said: "O King, your son acted as he did out of ignorance. From now on he will not commit such an impropriety. The prince should be pardoned for my sake. I am fully satisfied." After these words, the king released his son and the brahmin went home.

'After narrating this story, the genie asked: "O King, who was the more virtuous of the two?" "It was the king," said King Vikrama. But the silence had been broken with his words and, after hearing them, the genie went back to the śami tree.

'The king then returned to the tree and again took the genie on his shoulder. As he was coming back, the genie once more recounted a story, and in this manner he narrated twenty-five tales to the king.

'Finally, the genie was pleased on perceiving the king's virtues: his subtle intelligence and expertise in the arts, his compassion, courage and magnanimity. "O King," he said to Vikramaditya, "this naked yogi is trying to kill you." "How?" asked the king. The genie replied: "When you take me there, he will tell you, 'O King, you must be very tired. Now circumambulate this sacred fire, make obeisance with a prostration, and go home.' When you bow down to make the obeisance, the naked one will slay you with a sword. Then he will perform the fire sacrifice with your flesh and make me into a brahmin. By doing this he will gain the eight magic powers[5] such as lightness and the others."

'"What should I do?" asked the king. The genie said: "This is what you should do. When the naked one tells you to make obeisance and go, you should say: 'I am the sovereign. All the kings bow to me, but I have never bowed to anyone. So I do not know how to make obeisance. You must demonstrate it to me by doing it first.' And when he bows down to do so, you should cut off his head. I will do the fire sacrifice for you, and the eight magic powers will become yours.

'The king acted as the genie had directed. The latter turned into a brahmin and himself conducted the fire sacrifice, using the yogi's head for the final oblation. The king then obtained the eight magic powers.

'"I am pleased with you, O King," said the genie, "choose a boon." "If you are pleased," the king responded, "then bring this naked one back to life, And you must come to me whenever I call for you." The genie agreed, and went away to his abode after reviving the yogi. As for King Vikrama, he gave the eight magic powers to the naked ascetic, and returned to his capital.'

After telling this tale, the statuette said to King Bhoja: 'If you have such magnanimity, daring and other virtues, then sit on this throne, O King!' But the king remained silent.

32. The Image of Poverty

*W*ishing once again to ascend the great throne of Indra, King Bhoja came up to the thirty-second statuette, who surpassed all men in her extraordinary shrewdness. She clapped her hands and burst into laughter, saying: 'Great king, you have tremendous persistence in wanting to mount the throne of such a prince.' 'What was he like, good lady? Tell me,' said the monarch. 'Listen, O King,' she replied, her teeth sparkling like brilliant camphor, 'to a tale of high virtue of that man of accomplishment.

'When Bhartrihari became an ascetic, and retired to the forest[1], renouncing his kingdom which was rich with grain and treasure, King Vikramaditya took it over with the consent of all the ministers. Adorned with rare qualities, he ruled the land well, demonstrating constant righteousness and pleasing all the people, so that his fame spread throughout the world.

'The son of a merchant from a neighbouring village once came to trade in Avanti. Amazed to see the conditions there, he told his father on his return: "Father, whatever merchandise comes to Avanti is all purchased swiftly by its people; that which remains is bought in its entirety by nightfall by the king to prevent any aspersion that no one buys the things which come to the city."

'The father was a sharp operator. After listening to his son, he had an image made of iron, and named it Poverty. Then he went with it to Avanti, and stood on the highway, telling whoever asked him: "This is Poverty, which I have brought here for sale. The price is one thousand dināras."

'The image of Poverty had no takers whatsoever. But, in accordance with the king's orders, his officers took it in the evening after paying the price. Poverty was then placed in the treasury.

'The arrival of Poverty was noticed by the king's sevenfold Royal Fortune. That night Fortune appeared before the king in her septuple form, adorned with tinkling jewelled girdles and garlands. He got up hastily to propitiate the deity with bows and salutations, saying:

"Hail to Fortune! With her there,
all virtues are as good as present also;
and with her departure,
they too are as good as gone.

Hail forever to Fortune[2],
the ornament of the earth,
for engendering whom the ocean
is called the repository of jewels.

"Hail to Fortune, by union with whom
Krishna became renowned in the three worlds,
and whose offspring is Kāma,
the delighter of people."

'After praising her thus, the king enquired of Fortune why she had come in person. "King," she replied, "I am going away as Poverty has come into your treasury." "Goddess! Do not go!" the king exclaimed. "All the pleasures of this world depend upon your grace!" "In no way can I stay where Poverty exists," said Fortune. On hearing this, the king said: "Since the image of Poverty has been accepted by me, it must remain accepted. There are no two ways about it. If you must go, then go." And Fortune went away.'

'Then, within moments, there arrived Discrimination. "O King," said he, "we cannot stay where Poverty exists. Fortune has gone. I too am going." And though the king pressed him to stay, he also took leave and departed.'

'Again, within moments, there came Courage, and said to the king: "We cannot stay where Poverty exists. That is why Fortune and Discrimination have already gone. You and I have long been intimate. But now I have come to take leave, for I too must go."

'The king was perturbed. "Alas," he said to himself, "If Courage leaves man, then what is left? For,

Let Fortune go, she is fickle by nature;
let merits leave, with Discrimination
at their head; let Life depart too,
it is ever set to do so; but let
no man be forsaken by Courage.

'"O Courage," he then cried, "let even all the others go away, but you must not." "O King," Courage replied, 'In no way can I stay when Poverty is there." "In that case," said the king, "here is my head! Take it too. For, what is the use of living without you!" And, drawing his sword, as he was about to cut off his head, Courage caught hold of his hand.

'Then Courage remained with Vikrama, and his companions, Fortune and Discrimination, came back. Therefore, O King, sit on this throne if you have such courage.'

✜

Epilogue

After extolling the virtues of the noble Vikramaditya in two and thirty tales, the thirty-two moonstone statuettes appeared in the illustrious Bhoja's assembly as heavenly nymphs. Glorious to behold with tinkling earrings and other ornaments, they said: 'Thus was King Vikramaditya, O King Bhoja. You too are not ordinary. You both are incarnations of Nara and Nārāyaṇa, the divine sages of yore. You, King Bhoja, are pure of character, proficient in all the arts, and marked by generosity and other virtues. There is no king greater than you in this present age. By your grace our sins have been redeemed, and all thirty-two of us have been released from the curse.'

'How did your curse come about?' asked Bhoja. 'Tell me the story from the beginning.' 'King,' they replied, 'we are thirty-two celestial nymphs. Our names are[1] Jayā, Vijayā, Jayantī, Aparājita, Jayaghoshā, Manjughosā, Lilāvatī, Jayavatī, Jayasenā, Madanasenā, Madanamanjarī, Śringārakalikā, Rātipriyā, Naramohinī, Bhoganidhi, Prabhāvatī, Suprabhā, Chandramukhī, Anangadhvajā, Kuranganayanā, Lāvanyavatī, Saubhāgyamanjarī, Chandrikā, Hansagamanā, Vidyutprabhā, Ānandaprabhā, Chandrakāntā, Rūpakāntā, Surapriyā, Devānandā, Padmāvatī and Padminī.

'All of us are servants of the goddess Pārvatī. We were objects of her grace, and our hearts were filled with joy. Once we saw the handsome god, her consort, sitting upon his jewelled throne, and felt the desire to sleep with him. The goddess Pārvatī noticed this, and was infuriated. "You all will become lifeless statuettes on earth," she cursed us, "except that you will have the human skill of speech."

'We prostrated ourselves and begged that the curse be ended. The goddess has a tender and merciful heart. She said: "When Vikramaditya will have taken this throne .to earth, and when he dies after ruling from it for many years, this royal seat will be buried in a place of purity. Then it will come into the possession of King Bhoja, who will take it to his capital and install it there. Attempting to mount it, he will converse with you all, and you will recount to him the deeds of Vikramaditya. That is when this curse will terminate."

'This is why we obstructed your mounting this throne. It was for our release from the curse, securing which depended on your kindness. Now, thanks to you, it has taken place. We are pleased with you, O King; choose a boon.'

'What is it that I lack?' replied King Bhoja. 'I have everything. Even so, I will ask for something to benefit others. May the might, majesty and fame, the generosity and the steadfastness increase of all mortals who narrate or listen to the deeds of Vikramaditya. May these deeds remain forever famous on earth. And to those who fear them, may there never be any danger from ghosts, spectres and ghouls; sirens, witches and pestilence demons; ogres and suchlike; nor from snakes and other pests.'

'O King Bhoja,' said the former statuettes, 'it will be as you have said,' After granting this boon they returned to their abode.

Thereafter King Bhoja installed the throne in a marvellous shrine made of gold and the nine priceless gems, and established upon it the great god Śiva. He worshipped both with the sixteen offerings, and ruled the earth, protecting the institutions of society with his dharma.

Pārvatī was deeply contented on hearing this tale told by Parameśvara, the Supreme Lord.

Here end the tales of the
thirty-two statuettes.

✛

APPENDIX

✳

The Birth of Vikramaditya

*I*n the land of Gurjarī there is a forest between the rivers Mahilā and Sābhravatī which was ruled by the sage Tāmralipta. His daughter Yaśovatī and her husband, King Premasena, enjoyed all the pleasures of the world, and to them was born a girl, Madanarekhā, who grew up, waxing every day like the moon.

King Premasena had two pages named Deva Śarmā and Hari Śarmā respectively. The former would go to the river every day to wash the king's clothes. There he came to be addressed by some divine being who remained invisible, but spoke the language of men. This mysterious voice called daily from on high: 'What ho! Let that King Premasena marry his daughter to me. Otherwise it will not be good for him and his city.'

Deva Śarmā was wonderstruck. 'What could this be?' he thought. 'I see nothing, actually.' He reported the matter to the king, who observed: 'You are lying.' 'Sire,' responded the page, 'I will not go today. Send someone else to that place to wash the clothes.' The king then sent Hari Śarmā, who also heard the same voice and was filled with wonder. On his return he told the king what had happened.

Both boys had said: 'There is a mysterious voice there.' The king was amazed. The next time the page went to wash the clothes, he himself followed secretly. And, hiding behind a tree, he too heard the very same voice and words.

'What is this?' the king pondered, his mind full of doubt, 'Is it some god or is it a spirit?' On returning home he summoned the ministers, priests and other prominent persons, and asked: 'What shall we do? This voice at the river says: "Let King Premasena give his own daughter to me in marriage. In this way it will be well. Otherwise there will be trouble." Who it is, we do not know.'

'Master,' said the ministers and the priests, 'how can your daughter be given to someone unknown? Call him suitably, and ask him who he is.' The king then went to the river again, and the same voice uttered the same words. 'Are you a god or a demi-god, a demon or a man?' he asked. The being then appeared and said: 'King, I was Indra's chamberlain in the past. I lusted after the wives of others, and could not live without them. Many a time did Indra forbid me, but I would not stop. Eventually Indra cursed me, and I became an ass in the house of a potter in Your Majesty's city. At present I am roaming on the river bank. As such, I ask for your daughter. If you give her to me, all will be well for you. If not, there will be trouble for you and the people of the city.'

'I would give you my daughter if you were a god,' said the king. 'But how can I do that if you are an ass?' But the voice simply reiterated: 'Give her to me.'

Premasena feared for his city and, just to prevent anything untoward from happening, he decided to give his girl to the ass. But he asked once again: 'O chief of gods, if you have divine powers then build a wall of copper around the city, and also a palace with the thirty-two features where one may live.' The god did all this during the fourth watch of the night. Waking up in the morning, the people were astonished to see the copper rampart. It included on the highway a barrier which no one could open, so that all were perplexed.

The king was informed, and he too came to the barricaded highway and was amazed. He called in his

mind for the god, who appeared and said: 'O King, send
for the potter in whose house I live. The mere touch of his
hand will lift the barrier.' All the potters were then
summoned, but they fled in every direction, thinking:
'Perhaps the king is going to kill us on the highway.'
Thereafter the king sent only for the potter who kept the
ass, but he hid inside his house and had to be pulled out
forcibly by the officers who took him to the barricaded
highway. At the king's orders he opened it, to the delight
of the people as well as their ruler.

Meanwhile the girl Madanarekhā had heard that she
had been betrothed to an ass by the apprehensive king in
order to protect the people, his city and family. 'Alas!' she
said to herself, 'even if my heart bursts, what had to be has
happened. This is my karma.' The king married her to the
ass amidst great festivities, and she went to the palace built
by the god, where she remained lost in a trance.

The god now shed his asinine shape and, assuming a
divine form adorned with fragrant, pollen-laden blossoms
of the celestial pārijata and mandāra trees, he enjoyed all
the sensual delights with Madanarekhā. He did this every
day: sometimes on the Meru mountain, at others on the
Mānasa lake; sometimes in the cities of the demi-gods and
the demons, watching dances, and listening to music with
her, and indulging in all kinds of pleasures. She too was
supremely happy, and the attendants who accompanied
her kept all this secret. Several years passed thus.

Madanarekhā's mother used to worry about her
daughter living with an ass. She came to the palace one
day, and saw the god shedding his donkey hide as usual
and assuming a radiant form, after which he went into the
inner quarter. 'How fortunate and meritorious is my girl,
to have found such a husband!' the queen said to herself.
'I am blessed to have given birth to such a daughter.
Through her I too will earn merit.' Reflecting further, she
decided: 'I will throw this donkey skin into the fireplace,

so that he always keeps his present form.' Thinking thus, she threw the skin into the fire.

This was seen by Gandharvasena[1], for that was the name of the god turned into an ass. He told his wife: 'My dear, the duration of my curse is over, and the curse itself is ended. I am now going back to heaven.' 'What will happen to me?' she asked. 'I would come with you, if I was not carrying your child in my womb. Now what should I do?'

'Stay here in peace,' said the god. 'When the child is born, name him Vikramaditya. A child of mine is also there in the womb of your servant girl. He should be named Bhartrihari.' Having obtained release from the curse, the god then went away to heaven.

The queen told the king about what she had learnt. He called a soothsayer and asked what would happen to his daughter. 'She will have a son,' he said, 'and he will become the king.' This created an apprehension in Premasena's mind. 'So, the son of my daughter will become the king,' he thought, and he sent men to watch over the unborn child in Madanarekhā's womb. They mounted guard, and she wondered: 'Why have these men been posted to watch over my unborn child?'

Madanarekhā then told a flower girl who had come to her: 'Do something to protect and bring up my unborn child.' The flower seller agreed and brought a knife the following morning. With it Madanarekhā cut open her own belly and delivered her child to the flower girl. But she herself perished. The florist took the baby, along with Bhartrihari, the other child, and went with them to a village near Ujjayini. There she brought them up, and Vikrama grew day by day, together with Bhartrihari. 'A flower girl took away your daughter's child,' the king was informed. He had now lost both his daughter and her son; in that condition he named his city Stambhavati—the place benumbed[2]—and so it came to be known.

Notes

Introduction

1. *Alberuni's India*, tr. E.C. Sachau and ed. A.T. Embree, New York, 1971.

2. Edgerton. See Note 8 below.

3. By Nandlal Bose, described in the *Indian Express* of 12.1.1993

4. *History of Indian Literature* by M. Winternitz, tr. Subhadra Jha, Delhi, 1985. Referred to hereafter as Winternitz.

5. Edgerton. See Notes 8 and Appendix 1 below.

6. *Vikram and the Vampire*, tr. Sir Richard Burton, London, 1870.

7. Figures within brackets in this and the next paragraph refer to the Table of Contents numbers in the present book.

8. *Vikrama's Adventures* by Franklin Edgerton, Harvard Oriental Series, Volumes 26 and 27, Cambridge, 1926. Referred to here as Edgerton.

9. *The Kāvya-Portions in the Kathā-Literature,* Vol. II by Ludwik Sternbach, Meharchand Lachhmandas, Delhi, 1974. Referred to hereafter as Sternbach. This and Edgerton comprise the most detailed studies to date of the *Simhāsana Dvātriṃsikā.*

10. Sternbach.

11. Winternitz.

12. Edgerton.

13. Sternbach.

14. Sternbach.

15. Winternitz.

16. Sternbach.

17. The sources mentioned are among those traced in detail by Sternbach. Quotations traced by him to a few well-known works have been so identified in subsequent notes.

18. *A History of India*, Vol. I, by Romila Thapar, London, 1966.

19. Sternbach.

20. In *Glimpses of Sanskrit Literature*, ed. A.N.D. Haksar, New Delhi, 1995.

21. Sternbach.

22. *Stories of Vikramaditya (Simhāsana Dvātriṃsikā)* in English by V.A.K. Aiyer, Bombay 1960, contains very different material. It is also described as a retelling and does not specify its source.

23. Sternbach.

24. Winternitz.

25. These are tales 1, 3, 4, 13, 24 and 29. The introductory lines in the first two are drawn from SR, and in the other four from JR.

I. Prologue

1. The elephant-headed god, traditionally invoked at the beginning of an enterprise to keep it free of impediments.

2. The gods respectively of preservation, creation and destruction, and the goddess of learning.

3. This well known verse occurs in many works, including the *Panchatantra*, the *Hitopadeśa* and various Chānakya collections. Sternbach.

II. King Bhartrihari and the Fruit of Immortality

1. This verse occurs in the eighth century epic poem *Śiśupālavadha* by Māgha. Of the preceding four verses the first three are found in the *Hitopadeśa* and the *Panchatantra*, while the last is from *Bhartrihari Śatakam*. Sternbach.

2. The god of love and desire.

IV. Vikrama and the Wicked Yogi

1. The *Ramayana* story is well known.

2. This story summarizes the plot of the *Vetāla Panchaviṃśatikā*, mentioned in the Introduction. See also note 31.3.

3. Cf. tale 21.

V. Vikrama gains the Throne

1. The following five verses actually occur in a text on dancing entitled *Vasantārajīya*, quoted by the writer Katayavema in his commentary on Kalidasa's *Mālavikāgnimitra*; the last three occur in Act II of that play. Cf: the critical apparatus in Edgerton.

VI. Vikrama's Death and the hiding of the Throne

1. Some scholars place the site of this town on the river Ganga opposite modern Allahabad; others locate it on the river Godavari.

VII. The Discovery of the Throne

1. Author of *Nītisāra,* an eighth century work on governance.

VIII. The Minister's Tale

1. The following three verses are quotations from the *Rati Rahasya* of Kokkoka, a twelfth or thirteenth century work on erotics. Edgerton.

IX. The Minister's Tale continued

1. This verse recurs in tale 31.

2. This verse, ending in the famous maxim *vināśakāle viparītabuddhih,* is also found in the *Mahabharata,* the *Panchatantra* and the *Hitopadeśa.* Sternbach.

The Thirty-two Tales of the Throne

3. The Four Jewels

1. This verse ends in the well known maxim *vasudhaiva kutumbakam,* and is also found in the *Hitopadeśa,* the *Panchatantra* and various Chānakya anthologies. It is repeated at tale 17 in a slightly different form.

6. Distress and Deceit

1. The fourfold classification of women on the basis of their supposed physical and temperamental characteristics was traditional in later Indian erotic literature. Cf. Note VIII. 1 above.

2. The verse occurs in *Sarva Darśana Samgraha* of Mādhava (thirteenth or fourteenth century), and has been used to date the present work. Sternbach.

3. The three debts of man were considered as owed respectively to the gods, the seers, and the ancestors, and discharged through offering sacrifices, studying the scriptures, and begetting a son.

7. The Decapitated Duo

1. This refers to the Dāna Khaṇḍa section of the *Chaturvarga Chintāmaṇi* of Hemādri (thirteenth century). The author is also mentioned by name in some texts of SR. The reference has been used to date the present work. Sternbach.

8. The Filling of the Lake

1. A type of dance. The description is obviously that of the god Śiva as Natarāja or king of dancers. Bhairava and Parameśvara are also representations of Śiva. Lambodara is another name of the god Gaṇeśa. Cf. note I. 1.

9. A Courtesan Rescued

1. This and the following equally well known verse, also occur in the *Bhartrihari Śatakam*. Sternbach.

2. Of the Jyotisha Śāstra, on astronomy. These are Tantra, Horā and Samhitā, concerned respectively with astronomy, horoscopes and natural astrology. Cf. *A History of Sanskrit Literature* by A.B. Keith, Oxford, 1920.

3. See notes VIII. 1 and 6.1.

12. The Curse on the Callous Wife

1. A shell once used as the smallest unit of currency.

2. A famous ogre in mythology.

13. The Gift of Merit

1. The purāṇa sources of the next seven verses are still to be identified.

2. The holy trinity of Brahmā, Vishnu and Śiva. Edgerton.

3. The warrior caste.

4. *Brahmarākshasa* in Sanskrit. A person of the priestly caste transformed into a demon as punishment for transgression of his ordained duties.

15. A Friend Indeed

1. The chaplain's name in Trivikrama in tale 9, where he also seems to be an older man. Both names are taken here from SR.

2. The popular *Māgha Melā* bathing festival is still held every year at *Prayāga*, modern Allahabad, during this month which corresponds to December-January.

16. A Springtime Gift

1. The bakula (*mimusope elengi*) was said to flower when sprayed with a mouthful of wine by a good-looking girl. There are similar literary conceits about the breath from a girl's mouth, a stroke of her foot, and an embrace from her breast, which bring blossoms to the mango, the asoka and the red amaranth respectively.

18. Vikrama visits the Sun

1. That is, confined under the bridge built by Rama.

2. This proper noun is also used in referring to someone whose name is not known:

3. These are: ruby, pearl, coral, emerald, topaz, diamond, sapphire, garnet and cat's eye. Each gem is associated with a planet, and together they constitute an auspicious combination still used in Indian jewellery.

4. Equilibrium, energy and inertia; or tranquility, passion and ignorance.

19. The Visit to the Nether World

1. Krishna here refers by the god Vishnu, by another of whose incarnations the righteous giant king Bāli was tricked into gifting his earthly domain. Bāli was then made ruler of the nether world, and the god rewarded his merit by standing guard at his gate.

24. The Judgement of Śālivāhana

1. Of the mercantile caste.

2. This story elaborates on the tale in section VI, in relation to which, however, there are important differences of detail.

3. The references in this sentence are to various divine beings.

4. All four are mythological figures whose charity and renunciation were of heroic proportions. The last named is the *Mahabharata* character Karna.

5. Cf. tale 19.

6. Cf. tale 20.

25. The Halting of Saturn

1. A sixth century astronomer and astrologer, author of the work *Brihatsamhitā*. He divided the subject into

three sections, cf. note 9.2. The verse which follows is ascribed to him. Sternbach.

2.   The father of the hero Rama.

28.   The King stops Human Sacrifice

1.   Seven manifestations of the Mother Goddess who participated in the battle with the buffalo demon, as described in the *Śri Durgā Saptaśatī*.

2.   The verse is sourced to Kalidasa's *Śakuntalā* (5.7). Sternbach.

30.   The Magician's Reward

1.   Sourced to Kalidasa's *Kumārasambhava* (4.33): Sternbach.

31.   The Genie's Tale

1.   The *tripundra*, drawn with three parallel and horizontal lines, and worn by devotees of the god Śiva.

2.   The month corresponding to November-December.

3.   As with the story in section IV, this tale also summarizes the *Vetāla Panchvimśatikā*, another work featuring king Vikramaditya. The end here, however, provides a new twist.

4.   Characters in the *Mahabharata*. But this verse does not seem to occur in the epic.

5.   Cf. tale 21.

32.   The Image of Poverty

1.   Cf. section II.

2. Lakshmi, the goddess of fortune, was born from the ocean and (next verse) married the god Vishnu. In the latter's incarnation as Krishna, their son was Kāma, the god of love. These three verses addressed to Lakshmi are in Prākrit in the original.

Epilogue

1. These names are taken from JR. There are some variations in other recensions.

Appendix

1. Edgerton thought that this name should perhaps be Gardabhasena (cf. Gardabha = ass). He refers to the Jaina work *Kālakāchārya Kathānaka,* in which Vikramaditya's predecessor king is named Gardabhilla. The work tells how the latter was expelled by the Śakas from Ujjayini, which was reconquered by Vikrama, who established a new era to mark the occasion.

2. The name could also mean a place with pillars. Any connection with the town of Khambat in Gujarat remains to be traced, bearing in mind that this story begins in the land of Gurjarī.

PENGUIN CLASSICS

THE EPIC OF GILGAMESH

'Surpassing all other kings, heroic in stature,
brave scion of Uruk, wild bull on the rampage!
Gilgamesh the tall, magnificent and terrible'

Miraculously preserved on clay tablets dating back as much as four thousand years, the poem of Gilgamesh, king of Uruk, is the world's oldest epic, predating Homer by many centuries. The story tells of Gilgamesh's adventures with the wild man Enkidu, and of his arduous journey to the ends of the earth in quest of the Babylonian Noah and the secret of immortality. Alongside its themes of family, friendship and the duties of kings, *The Epic of Gilgamesh* is, above all, about mankind's eternal struggle with the fear of death.

The Babylonian version has been known for over a century, but linguists are still deciphering new fragments in Akkadian and Sumerian. Andrew George's gripping translation brilliantly combines these into a fluent narrative and will long rank as the definitive English *Gilgamesh*.

'This masterly new verse translation' *The Times*

Translated with an introduction by Andrew George

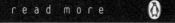

PENGUIN CLASSICS

THE ANALECTS CONFUCIUS

'The Master said, "If a man sets his heart on benevolence, he will be free from evil"'

The Analects are a collection of Confucius's sayings brought together by his pupils shortly after his death in 497 BC. Together they express a philosophy, or a moral code, by which Confucius, one of the most humane thinkers of all time, believed everyone should live. Upholding the ideals of wisdom, self-knowledge, courage and love of one's fellow man, he argued that the pursuit of virtue should be every individual's supreme goal. And while following the Way, or the truth, might not result in immediate or material gain, Confucius showed that it could nevertheless bring its own powerful and lasting spiritual rewards.

This edition contains a detailed introduction exploring the concepts of the original work, a bibliography and glossary and appendices on Confucius himself, *The Analects* and the disciples who compiled them.

Translated with an introduction and notes by D. C. Lau

PENGUIN CLASSICS

THE KORAN

'God is the light of the heavens and the earth . . . God guides to His light whom he will'

The Koran is universally accepted by Muslims to be the infallible Word of God as first revealed to the Prophet Muhammad by the Angel Gabriel nearly fourteen hundred years ago. Its 114 chapters, or *sūrahs*, recount the narratives central to Muslim belief, and together they form one of the world's most influential prophetic works and a literary masterpiece in its own right. But above all, the Koran provides the rules of conduct that remain fundamental to the Muslim faith today: prayer, fasting, pilgrimage to Mecca and absolute faith in God.

N. J. Dawood's masterly translation is the result of his life-long study of the Koran's language and style, and presents the English reader with a fluent and authoritative rendering, while reflecting the flavour and rhythm of the original. This edition follows the traditional sequence of the Koranic *sūrahs*.

'Across the language barrier Dawood captures the thunder and poetry of the original' *The Times*

Over a million copies sold worldwide.

Revised translation with an introduction and notes by N. J. Dawood

PENGUIN CLASSICS

THE BHAGAVAD GITA

'In death thy glory in heaven, in victory thy glory on earth.
Arise therefore, Arjuna, with thy soul ready to fight'

The Bhagavad Gita is an intensely spiritual work that forms the
cornerstone of the Hindu faith, and is also one of the masterpieces of
Sanskrit poetry. It describes how, at the beginning of a mighty battle
between the Pandava and Kaurava armies, the god Krishna gives
spiritual enlightenment to the warrior Arjuna, who realizes that the
true battle is for his own soul.

Juan Mascaró's translation of *The Bhagavad Gita* captures the
extraordinary aural qualities of the original Sanskrit. This edition
features a new introduction by Simon Brodbeck, which discusses
concepts such as dehin, prakriti and Karma.

'The task of truly translating such a work is indeed formidable. The
translator must at least possess three qualities. He must be an artist in
words as well as a Sanskrit scholar, and above all, perhaps, he must be
deeply sympathetic with the spirit of the original. Mascaró has succeeded
so well because he possesses all these' *The Times Literary Supplement*

Translated by Juan Mascaró with an introduction by Simon Brodbeck

Penguin Classics

BUDDHIST SCRIPTURES

'Whoever gives something for the good of others, with heart full of sympathy, not heeding his own good, reaps unspoiled fruit'

While Buddhism has no central text such as the Bible or the Koran, there is a powerful body of scripture from across Asia that encompasses the *dharma*, or the teachings of Buddha. This rich anthology brings together works from a broad historical and geographical range, and from languages such as Pali, Sanskrit, Tibetan, Chinese and Japanese. There are tales of the Buddha's past lives, a discussion of the qualities and qualifications of a monk, and an exploration of the many meanings of Enlightenment. Together they provide a vivid picture of the Buddha and of the vast nature of the Buddhist tradition.

This new edition contains many texts presented in English for the first time as well as new translations of some well-known works, and also includes an informative introduction and prefaces to each chapter by scholar of Buddhism Donald S. Lopez Jr, with suggestions for further reading and a glossary.

Edited with an introduction by Donald S. Lopez, Jr

PENGUIN CLASSICS

THE RUBA'IYAT OF OMAR KHAYYAM

'Many like you come and many go
Snatch your share before you are snatched away'

Revered in eleventh-century Persia as an astronomer, mathematician and
philosopher, Omar Khayyam is now known first and foremost for his
Ruba'iyat. The short epigrammatic stanza form allowed poets of his day to
express personal feelings, beliefs and doubts with wit and clarity, and
Khayyam became one of its most accomplished masters with his touching
meditations on the transience of human life and of the natural world. One
of the supreme achievements of medieval literature, the reckless
romanticism and the pragmatic fatalism in the face of death means these
verses continue to hold the imagination of modern readers.

In this translation, Persian scholar Peter Avery and the poet John Heath-
Stubbs have collaborated to recapture the sceptical, unorthodox spirit of
the original by providing a near literal English version of the original
verse. This edition also includes a map, appendices, bibliography and an
introduction examining the *ruba'i* form and Khayyam's life and times.

'[Has] restored to that masterpiece all the fun, dash and vivacity.'
Jan Morris

Translated by Peter Avery and John Heath-Stubbs

PENGUIN CLASSICS

THE ODYSSEY HOMER

'I long to reach my home and see the day of my return. It is my never-failing wish'

The epic tale of Odysseus and his ten-year journey home after the Trojan War forms one of the earliest and greatest works of Western literature. Confronted by natural and supernatural threats – shipwrecks, battles, monsters and the implacable enmity of the sea-god Poseidon – Odysseus must test his bravery and native cunning to the full if he is to reach his homeland safely and overcome the obstacles that, even there, await him.

E. V. Rieu's translation of *The Odyssey* was the very first Penguin Classic to be published, and has itself achieved classic status. For this edition, his text has been sensitively revised and a new introduction added to complement E. V. Rieu's original introduction.

'One of the world's most vital tales ... *The Odyssey* remains central to literature' Malcolm Bradbury

Translated by E. V. Rieu
Revised translation by D. C. H. Rieu, with an introduction by Peter Jones

PENGUIN CLASSICS

THE ILIAD   HOMER

'Look at me. I am the son of a great man. A goddess was my mother. Yet death and inexorable destiny are waiting for me'

One of the foremost achievements in Western literature, Homer's *Iliad* tells the story of the darkest episode in the Trojan War. At its centre is Achilles, the greatest warrior-champion of the Greeks, and his refusal to fight after being humiliated by his leader Agamemnon. But when the Trojan Hector kills Achilles's close friend Patroclus, he storms back into battle to take revenge – although knowing this will ensure his own early death. Interwoven with this tragic sequence of events are powerfully moving descriptions of the ebb and flow of battle, of the domestic world inside Troy's besieged city of Ilium, and of the conflicts between the gods on Olympus as they argue over the fate of mortals.

E. V. Rieu's acclaimed translation of Homer's *Iliad* was one of the first titles published in Penguin Classics, and now has classic status itself. For this edition, Rieu's text has been revised, and a new introduction and notes by Peter Jones complement the original introduction.

Translated by E. V. Rieu
Revised and updated by Peter Jones with D. C. H. Rieu
Edited with an introduction and notes by Peter Jones

PENGUIN CLASSICS

THE RISE OF THE ROMAN EMPIRE   POLYBIUS

'If history is deprived of the truth, we are left with nothing but an idle, unprofitable tale.'

In writing his account of the relentless growth of the Roman Empire, the Greek statesman Polybius (*c.* 200–118 BC) set out to help his fellow-countrymen understand how their world came to be dominated by Rome. Opening with the Punic War in 264 BC, he vividly records the critical stages of Roman expansion: its campaigns throughout the Mediterranean, the temporary setbacks inflicted by Hannibal and the final destruction of Carthage in 146 BC. An active participant in contemporary politics, as well as a friend of many prominent Roman citizens, Polybius was able to draw on a range of eyewitness accounts and on his own experiences of many of the central events, giving his work immediacy and authority.

Ian Scott-Kilvert's translation fully preserves the clarity of Polybius's narrative. This substantial selection of the surviving volumes is accompanied by an introduction by F. W. Walbank, which examines Polybius's life and times, and the sources and technique he employed in writing his history.

Translated by Ian Scott-Kilvert
Selected with an introduction by F. W. Walbank

PENGUIN CLASSICS

THE PERSIAN EXPEDITION   XENOPHON

'The only things of value which we have at present are our arms and our courage'

In *The Persian Expedition*, Xenophon, a young Athenian noble who sought his destiny abroad, provides an enthralling eyewitness account of the attempt by a Greek mercenary army – the Ten Thousand – to help Prince Cyrus overthrow his brother and take the Persian throne. When the Greeks were then betrayed by their Persian employers, they were forced to march home through hundreds of miles of difficult terrain – adrift in a hostile country and under constant attack from the unforgiving Persians and warlike tribes. In this outstanding description of endurance and individual bravery, Xenophon, one of those chosen to lead the retreating army, provides a vivid narrative of the campaign and its aftermath, and his account remains one of the best pictures we have of Greeks confronting a 'barbarian' world.

Rex Warner's distinguished translation captures the epic quality of the Greek original and George Cawkwell's introduction sets the story of the expedition in the context of its author's life and tumultuous times.

Translated by Rex Warner with an introduction by George Cawkwell

THE STORY OF PENGUIN CLASSICS

Before 1946 ... 'Classics' are mainly the domain of academics and students, without readable editions for everyone else. This all changes when a little-known classicist, E. V. Rieu, presents Penguin founder Allen Lane with the translation of Homer's *Odyssey* that he has been working on and reading to his wife Nelly in his spare time.

1946 *The Odyssey* becomes the first Penguin Classic published, and promptly sells three million copies. Suddenly, classic books are no longer for the privileged few.

1950s Rieu, now series editor, turns to professional writers for the best modern, readable translations, including Dorothy L. Sayers's *Inferno* and Robert Graves's *The Twelve Caesars*, which revives the salacious original.

1960s The Classics are given the distinctive black jackets that have remained a constant throughout the series's various looks. Rieu retires in 1964, hailing the Penguin Classics list as 'the greatest educative force of the 20th century'.

1970s A new generation of translators arrives to swell the Penguin Classics ranks, and the list grows to encompass more philosophy, religion, science, history and politics.

1980s The Penguin American Library joins the Classics stable, with titles such as *The Last of the Mohicans* safeguarded. Penguin Classics now offers the most comprehensive library of world literature available.

1990s The launch of Penguin Audiobooks brings the classics to a listening audience for the first time, and in 1999 the launch of the Penguin Classics website takes them online to a larger global readership than ever before.

The 21st Century Penguin Classics are rejacketed for the first time in nearly twenty years. This world famous series now consists of more than 1300 titles, making the widest range of the best books ever written available to millions – and constantly redefining the meaning of what makes a 'classic'.

The Odyssey continues ...

The best books ever written

PENGUIN (🐧) CLASSICS

SINCE 1946

Find out more at www.penguinclassics.com